The Cataphract Errant

Marc Edmond Best

CHAPTER 1

The *Huntress* marched for Kingsforge.

The towering machine strode across the alchemically-treated stone of the cataphract road, each footfall sending tremors through the ground. Though her white-enameled armor was dented and even torn in places from her previous battles, the damage was only cosmetic, as her pace never slowed, her stride never faltered, and the blue smoke from her back-mounted exhaust vents kept billowing out in a steady stream.

The *Huntress* had her visor open, allowing the woman at helm better visibility (as well as a pleasant breeze on her face). Lady Diana Fenvale dressed the part of a Cataphract captain in a proudly plumed hat and a maroon doublet with the *Huntress'* leaping hound sigil embroidered on its left breast. She sat at the *Huntress'* controls with confident familiarity, as if she'd been born to them. In a sense, she had been: the *Huntress* had belonged to the Fenvales for generations, and she was the latest of her line to operate the great machine.

The *Huntress'* passing drew attention. Which was entirely understandable; a three-story-tall war machine that walked like a man was impossible to miss. Farmers came out to gawp at the *Huntress* as she passed, and other travelers hurried to the side of the road to give them the right of way. Ostensibly, yielding to passing Cataphracts was meant to honor the noble piloting them, but there was a far more practical reason to get out of the way of a walking war machine taller than most houses.

Few of the onlookers paid any attention to the man following behind.

Victor Brinden, a bespectacled, nervy man in a cloth cap, sat in the saddle of a humble workhorse, leading two more heavily-laden pack horses by a rope lead. He followed a safe distance behind the *Huntress*, all the better to keep an eye on the *Huntress'* workings.

With a trained eye, Victor studied the *Huntress* in motion, searching for any stiffness in her gait, any indication that he might have made a mistake while restoring her. The *Huntress* had performed excellently during her recent battle with the *Guilt of Gold*, another Duelist-sized Cataphract, but the simple march was even more of a test. A long period of steady, repetitive motion could put a different kind of stress on a Cataphract's workings in a way that heated battle didn't. Victor couldn't see any problems in the *Huntress*' steady stride, which only made him imagine new and inventive problems that he had somehow missed. Instead of pride at seeing the *Huntress* cover ground so easily, Victor only felt his palms itching to work on the *Huntress* once again, to ensure that she was working at peak efficiency, down to the last bolt.

Rounding out the unlikely caravan was a dog big enough to be mistaken for a small pony at a far enough distance. Lily trotted happily alongside Victor's horse, easily keeping up with the the Cataphract's pace, as hackleback mastiffs had been bred to do generations earlier. Every so often she would bound off into the woods and fields alongside the road, often returning with a squirrel or rabbit dangling from her jaws and a proud spring to her step.

They'd been traveling like this for days; Lady Fenvale marched for as long as the light held and had the *Huntress* powered up before the sun fully crested the horizon. By the time they set up camp each night (it was always a camp, as Lady Fenvale purposefully avoided the inns and roadhouses), Victor had little time or energy for anything beyond the most superficial of inspections. Despite Victor's anxiety, the *Huntress* held up against the monotonous wear and tear of the march.

Once they reached the flat, solid expanse of the Cataphract road, they covered more and more ground each day. The alchemy-treated stone of the road offered better footing for the *Huntress*, as well as an excuse for Lady Fenvale to press her harder.

Victor watched one landscape blur into another as they left the thick pines and oaks of Lady Fenvale's home and emerged out into the wheat-laden farmland of the interior. On the afternoon of the seventh (or possibly eighth, Victor had lost track) day of hard travel, the *Huntress* abruptly stopped in the middle of the Cataphract road.

4

Fearing some sort of malfunction, Victor rode his horse around in front of the Cataphract and waved his hat at Lady Fenvale as she opened her machine's visor.

"What's wrong?" Victor's voice cracked, dry from road dust and sudden fear. He searched the *Huntress* for any signs of damage. "It's not the right knee, is it? I knew the motive gears needed more calibration—"

"The *Huntress* is fine," Lady Fenvale yelled back. "But you might want to get out of the way."

"What for?" Victor put his hat back on.

"Look." Lady Fenvale leaned out of the *Huntress'* open visor and pointed further down the road. Victor turned in his saddle—and then nearly fell out of it once he saw what Lady Fenvale pointed to. Miles down the road, a whole squadron of Cataphracts approached. Victor had known it was only a matter of time before they ran into another machine, but he hadn't expected so many.

Two slender skirmishers led the way, red pennants flapping from their long lances. A pair of duelists, each the size of the *Huntress*, followed behind, their intricately etched armor and armaments gleaming with fresh polish. And behind them loomed an enormous siegebreaker, its armored shoulders wide enough that it blocked the whole of the Cataphract road. The siegebreaker carried no weapon; it didn't have to. With fists the size of farmhouses, the metal titan could wrench a smaller Cataphract limb from limb with hardly any effort at all.

"Recognize any of them?" Lady Fenvale called down from her perch.

At such a distance, there was only one sigil Victor could identify. The siegebreaker's breastplate bore an engraving of a parchment scroll, rolled into a tube and sealed with red ribbon.

"That's—that's *King Leopold's Pardon*." Victor tried to keep his voice steady, with arguable success.

"I suspected as much, but I wasn't sure," Lady Fenvale said.

Victor swallowed. *King Leopold's Pardon* was one of the oldest Cataphracts—one of the first Cataphracts. As the story went, captaining a Cataphract wasn't always seen as an honor. In fact, in the early days of the Behemoth Age, it could be viewed as a particularly complicated way to commit suicide. Eventually, one would either die to a marauding Behemoth, or die from the countless number of things that could go wrong on such an enormous and complicated piece of machinery. The first Cataphracts were notoriously dangerous, lacking the countless improvements that had been made to their design and workings over the years. One could fall from the helm-seat, or crushed in the workings of its gears, or cooked alive by superheated smoke if the alchemical furnace was ruptured.

And so, King Leopold started offering commissions to condemned prisoners willing to take the risk of helming the war machine, which was how *King Leopold's Pardon* earned her name. Ironically, she proved to be surprisingly reliable for such an early model, and soon captaining *King Leopold's Pardon* came to be an honor to be awarded to the bravest and most loyal (or at least the best-connected) scions of the noble houses. *King Leopold's Pardon* became an extension of the monarch's will, and now she'd been dispatched with the squadron to meet the *Huntress*.

Victor tightened his grip on his reins, unsure if *King Leopold's Pardon* had come to escort Lady Fenvale—or arrest her.

"You're not going to try to fight them, are you?" Victor asked.

"Only if I have to," Lady Fenvale said with her typically unshakable bravado. "Which is why you need to get out of the way."

The road shook with the rhythmic beat of the oncoming squadron's footsteps, and Victor steered his mount and the packhorses over to the side of the road. Lily followed without being told, showing far more confidence than the nervous horses.

"Victor!" Lady Fenvale leaned precariously far over the lip of the *Huntress'* open visor. "If things go badly, take Lily and run for Fenvale Manor. Turquo will give you safe haven."

"I hope it won't come to that," Victor said, with all honesty.

"So do I." Lady Fenvale dropped back into her helm-seat, then pulled on a control lever to make the *Huntress* raise one hand in greeting.

The Cataphract squadron closed in.

Victor had thought he'd gotten used to feeling the thundering footsteps of a Cataphract through his boots, but the sheer tonnage of so many huge machines marching in lockstep was enough to rattle every bone in his body.

The Cataphracts fanned out to the sides of the road as they closed in. The skirmishers bounded past the *Huntress*, one taking up a position further down the road, the other coming to stand alarmingly close to Victor's own position. In turn, the duelists focused on Lady Fenvale, flanking her. They kept their poleaxes in parade position, held diagonally across their chests. It wasn't overtly threatening (insomuch as an axe with a blade as big as a banquet table could be nonthreatening), but they remained ready for battle nonetheless.

King Leopold's Pardon loomed over the *Huntress*, but Lady Fenvale stood her ground, not moving to attack or retreat. She stared out of her Cataphract's open visor, and soon *King Leopold's Pardon* opened hers in turn.

A large man with an equally large collection of medals pinned to his chest stood up at the siegebreaker's helm. "Explain yourself!"

"I am Lady Diana Fenvale, captain of the *Huntress*. I march for Kingsforge, to take the Cataphract Oath," Lady Fenvale replied, her own voice carrying clearly. "Who dares stand in my way?"

A pregnant silence fell over the stretch of road. At his distance, Victor couldn't see how the siegebreaker's captain responded. He thought about rummaging his spyglass out again, but the presence of the nearby skirmisher made him hesitate. Victor warily looked over at the lanky machine (the *Bearbaiter*, by the name engraved across her breastplate) and noted how long her slender leg struts were. Based on the estimated length of the *Bearbaiter*'s stride, Victor ran a few rough calculations in his head to figure the skirmisher's potential top speed. If he abandoned the packhorses and drove his own mount into a gallop, Victor concluded he might be able to elude the squadron. Maybe.

He hoped it wouldn't come to that.

Finally, the captain of *King Leopold's Pardon* replied. "You've made a mistake, Lady Fenvale."

"Have I?" Lady Fenvale asked. The *Huntress* shifted her stance slightly, readying to spring into action.

"My name is Cecil Barrowgale—General Barrowgale, if you want to be official about it. I'm not here to block your way, but to escort you. It's been a long time since anyone's taken the Cataphract Oath, so His Majesty has decided it should be done with all due ceremony. It is both my duty and my honor to accompany you to the capital." *King Leopold's Pardon* stepped back and to the side, then bowed at the waist. That the general could make such a gesture look graceful in a five-story-tall war machine was a subtle showcase of his skill at the helm, not to mention the construction of the siegebreaker. "Will you accept my hospitality, Lady Fenvale?"

"General, I would be honored."

CHAPTER 2

The *Huntress* fell into formation with the rest of the squadron, marching along as if she'd drilled with them for years. Victor couldn't help but notice how they kept the *Huntress* in the center of the formation. It could have been an honor, or General Barrowgale could have wanted to keep her surrounded. At least they'd allowed the *Huntress* to remain armed with her massive broadsword, though how much good even that weapon would do against a whole squadron was debatable.

In turn, the *Bearbaiter* "politely" led Victor and Lily to the squadron's supply train, situated further down the road. It was a small caravan, only about a dozen wagons of equipment and a small detachment of light cavalry to act as scouts and escorts.

Once the Cataphracts marched by, the wagons and horses creaked into motion and slowly started to follow, albeit at a much slower pace than Victor had been traveling for the last few days. He rode alongside the wagons, with Lily trotting along at his horse's heels. The other engineers recognized Victor as one of their own and bombarded him with questions during the trip.

"So that's really the *Huntress*, ay?"

"How'd you get her running? I thought she'd been scrapped after Osterbridge."

"Where's the rest of your crew?"

"Is that a hackleback mastiff?"

"You've read Pirondetti's latest paper, haven't you?"

"What kind of output are you getting out of her furnace? That's more smoke than I'd expect from a duelist the *Huntress*' size."

"Want a drink?"

At least that was easy to answer. Victor gulped down a half a jug of small beer and replied to the other queries as best he could. He spoke truthfully, for the most part. He omitted the details of where he'd acquired certain components, or how Lady Fenvale had tested the *Huntress* out by trouncing the *Guilt of Gold*. Thankfully, the other engineers didn't pry too much into the *Huntress'* immediate history once Victor got them talking on the more academic matters of her performance. Performance which was invariably compared to that of the other Cataphracts in the squadron. It wasn't long before each engineer started bragging and singing the praises of whichever Cataphract they worked on. Sometimes literally, as *King Leopold's Pardon* had been around long enough to feature heavily in more than a few ballads.

The whole caravan agreed that *King Leopold's Pardon* was the strongest Cataphract of the squadron, but the crews of the *Bearbaiter* and her fellow skirmisher the *Kestrel* kept a running bet on which one was faster. Likewise, there was a running debate over the fact that the *Swordbreaker* had fought in more battles, even if her fellow duelist the *Mad Tiger* had marched in more campaigns. Or perhaps it was the other way around—Victor soon lost track of the rapid-fire exchange of playful boasts, insults, and rattled-off statistics. The one thing all the men and women of the engineering crews could agree on was that their squadron was the finest in all of Leovaix, and therefore the finest in the world. Though Victor knew that any alchemical engineer worth their calipers would likely make similar claims, especially if they worked on as venerable a Cataphract as *King Leopold's Pardon*.

Hours passed, and miles went with them, at least for a little while. Abruptly, the squadron stopped in front of a large manor house perched beside the Cataphract road. The drovers swore and reined in their teams, and Victor did the same.

"We're stopping?" Victor leaned sideways in his saddle to get a better look ahead, but the hulking mass of *King Leopold's Pardon* blocked his view. "Is something wrong?"

"Wrong?" A grizzled engineer hopped off the wagon he'd been riding in. "Nothing's wrong. We're just stopping for the night."

Victor held a hand up to his eyes and squinted westward. "But it won't be dark for a few hours yet."

"Which should give the general plenty of time to talk to the duchess." The engineer gave a knowing laugh.

"With who?" Victor said.

"Duchess Rosalind. The general always stops at her estate when he's out on the march to … socialize." The engineer winked at Victor.

"But … Lady Fenvale is headed to Kingsforge. She's going to take the Cataphract Oath."

"So?" The engineer shrugged. "The city's not going anywhere. Neither's the king, ay? Besides, that lady of yours is lucky; the general will formally introduce her to Duchess Rosalind. She's a good person to know, they say. Connected. See?"

"Ah. Of course." Victor vaguely remembered hearing the Rosalinds' name somewhere or another, but as far as he knew the family didn't own a Cataphract.

The other engineer pointed to the manor house, where a sizable procession had gathered to greet the Cataphract captains. Though the supply train was still quite far from the house itself, Victor could still see how expensively they were dressed, the bright purples and yellows of their silk finery standing out at a distance. An older, dark-haired woman stood at the head of the group; from the size of her ruffled lace collar, Victor presumed it was Duchess Rosalind herself.

"And if we're lucky, we'll get invited inside as well." The engineer rubbed his hands in anticipation. "Duchess Rosalind's got the best cooks you'll find this side of the Lastwall Mountains. Biggest wine cellar, too."

"I'll keep that in mind." Movement caught Victor's eye, and he looked over to see *King Leopold's Pardon* lumber to the side of the road and settle into a kneel, smoke cutting off from her exhaust vents as her alchemical furnace shut down. The siegebreaker's visor opened, and General Barrowgale threw down a long rope ladder to make his descent.

The rest of the squadron followed his example, lining their Cataphracts in a row before shutting off their furnaces and climbing down to meet Duchess Rosalind and her entourage. "But in the meanwhile, I'd better take a look at the *Huntress*. Make sure that nothing's come loose during the march."

"Need help?" the engineer asked. "I wouldn't mind getting a look at your Cataphract's insides. See how she stacks up 'gainst the *Mad Tiger*."

"Ah, no, thank you," Victor said, if a beat too quickly. "It'll be easier if I do it myself. More relaxing, too."

"All right, just don't get too distracted, or you'll miss the duchess' banquet."

"I'll try."

Victor spurred his horse on and rode the short distance to where the squadron had settled in. Lily trotted a little ways ahead of Victor's horse, as if heading towards the Cataphracts was her idea. Several other engineers and journeymen from the supply train joined him, fanning out to check on their own machines.

By the time Victor got to the *Huntress*, a small crowd had gathered around Lady Fenvale. The tall swordswoman smiled and chatted with Duchess Rosalind, General Barrowgale, and several more important-looking individuals who Victor couldn't identify. The *Huntress*' captain looked far more at ease than she had at Maldrinne Manor. With a sword on her hip and a Cataphract at her command, Lady Fenvale was undoubtedly in her element. Upon seeing her mistress, Lily perked her ears and bounded ahead, muscling several servants out of the way. This earned a fresh round of cheery laughter from the assembled nobles. One delightedly giggly voice could be heard over the others.

"Lily! You've gotten so big!"

The dog wagged her tail.

Victor sighed in relief to see things going relatively well, then dismounted near the *Huntress*. He left Lady Fenvale to her socializing and set about reviewing her Cataphract for wear from so many days of travel. To his relief (and mild surprise), Victor found everything in order. Admittedly, the *Huntress'* legs were spattered with dried mud, and the patched and unpainted sections of her armor looked all the more piecemeal when flanked by the polished armor of the *Swordbreaker* and the *Mad Tiger*. But those were just cosmetic matters. As Victor pored over the Cataphract, he found the *Huntress'* plating still bolted in tight, her control cables still taut, and her motive gears still aligned; she was ready to fight at a moment's notice. Victor ran a hand over the sun-warmed metal of the *Huntress'* ankle plating and looked up at her. All it would take was a little paint and polish (or, well, a lot of paint and polish, Victor admitted) and the *Huntress* would fit right in with her shining, glorious counterparts.

"—and this is my chief engineer, Victor Brinden." Lady Fenvale's voice snapped Victor out of his daydreaming. He turned around to find himself facing a small crowd. Victor yanked his hat off and bowed as gallantly as he could manage. The feeling of so many eyes upon him made him suddenly aware of every grease spot and sweat stain dotting his travel clothes.

"Victor, this is the Duchess Rosalind, and her daughter, Lady Rosalind." Lady Fenvale gestured to an impressively ruffed noblewoman and a pale, petite woman about Lady Fenvale's own age. Lily leaned against the younger woman, happily wagging her tail as she had her ears scratched.

"A pleasure," Duchess Rosalind said, and her daughter nodded politely in turn.

"An honor to meet you, Your Grace. Thank you for your hospitality," said Victor.

"I should be the one thanking you, Master Brinden." Duchess Rosalind looked up at the *Huntress* with a wan smile. "Count Fenvale loved this machine. And so does his daughter. To think that you were able to single-handedly repair the *Huntress* after so many years, 'tis quite a feat. It's almost enough to make one wish the Rosalinds had a Cataphract of our own for you to work on."

"Th-thank you, Your Grace." Victor bowed again, both out of politeness and to hide the slight, embarrassed flush that ran up his cheeks. "If I can ever be of service, all you have to do is ask."

"I'll keep that in mind," Duchess Rosalind said with a casual flutter of her hand fan. Victor stood up just in time to see Lady Fenvale roll her eyes, while the duchess' daughter hid an amused giggle behind her silk-gloved hand.

"I'd appreciate it if you didn't tempt away my chief engineer." Only the slightest smile at the corner of Lady Fenvale's mouth betrayed the dry humor in her tone.

"If I were tempting him, he'd know," the duchess said. Lady Rosalind laughed again, looking over at Lady Fenvale as if sharing an inside joke.

"That's what I'm afraid of." Lady Fenvale shook her head. "In the meanwhile, I've some business to attend to before dinner, if you'd give us a moment."

"Of course, of course!" Duchess Rosalind said. "But don't keep us waiting. I've had my staff working on a proper reception for you ever since we got word of your accomplishments. It'd be a shame if you missed it."

"Which is why I won't," said Lady Fenvale.

"I'll hold you to that." Duchess Rosalind's voice carried playful authority. "Ta-ta!" she said, then turned about, and her various attendants and handmaidens scurried into formation behind her. Lady Rosalind ran her gloved hand down Lily's broad shoulder one last time and wordlessly looked up at Lady Fenvale before she moved to take her place in the procession by her mother.

Lady Fenvale remained quiet as she watched them go.

"They seem … nice?" Victor offered, breaking the silence.

"The Rosalinds have been friends and allies to the Fenvales for generations. Which is why my cousin didn't invite them to his fiasco of a Summer's Steel festival, I imagine. I've known Sophia—" She stopped herself , then took a deep breath before continuing. "—

I've known Lady Rosalind since the both of us were children. We're safe here. Relax."

"I'm not sure if I'm physically capable of relaxation anymore," Victor said.

"Try." Lady Fenvale smiled and patted Victor on the shoulder. "After all our—all your hard work, the *Huntress* walks again. Once I take the Cataphract Oath, my cousin won't have any more power over me. No more insults. No more threats. No more plays commissioned to make me look like a fool."

"He can still do all of those things once you take the Cataphract Oath," Victor noted. "As far as I understand, all the oath means is that he won't be able to lay a legal claim on the *Huntress*. Which, I might add, is an entirely admirable goal, but it won't be the end of our—your problems, Lady Fenvale."

"True. But here's the thing, Victor. There will always be new problems." Lady Fenvale leaned back on her heels and looked proudly up at the *Huntress*. "It's just that most problems look smaller from the helm of a Cataphract."

"I'm afraid I don't have the luxury of that perspective," Victor said.

"A fair point." Lady Fenvale nodded. A brief silence hung between them, until Lady Fenvale went on. "Tonight, while I dine with the Rosalinds, would you stay here and keep an eye on Lily? I'd rather not have her being a pest during the banquet."

Lily looked up at the sound of her name and let her mouth hang open in a toothy, canine smile. She dragged her long tongue over her muzzle, as if in anticipation of the delicacies she could beg, steal, or scavenge from the banquet table.

"I can see how that might be a concern," Victor said. "I'll be happy to. It'll give me time to tend to the *Huntress*. And, well, after everything that happened at Maldrinne Manor, I'm not quite in the mood for fine dining. Honestly, I thought you'd feel the same way."

"Normally, you'd be right. But Lady Rosalind and I are … close. I'm looking forward to the opportunity to catch up. I had

15

planned on stopping here anyway, even if we didn't have an escort." Lady Fenvale's fingers found a sensitive spot behind Lily's ear, and the big dog let out a contented grunt as she leaned into the attention. "Besides, there won't be a play this time."

"Sounds promising."

"I should be back before it gets too late. I'll bring some leftovers from the banquet."

"You don't have to do that—"

"For Lily."

"Ah."

CHAPTER 3

On the other side of the Cataphract road, sounds of music and laughter echoed from the open windows of Duchess Rosalind's manor house. More than a few engineers from the rest of the squadron made their way towards the sounds of revelry. Seeing as they weren't turned away, Victor assumed they'd found someplace to enjoy the Duchess' hospitality.

Victor contented himself with a dinner of hard cheese and dried sausage, washing it all down with a small jug of beer. Belly full and cheeks flushed, Victor strung up a hammock between the *Huntress'* ankles and settled in for an early night's sleep, while Lily hunkered down on the ground beneath him.

He woke the next morning with nothing to do. He had taken care of the *Huntress'* maintenance the night before, and without a proper workshop he didn't have the tools or resources to perform anything more involved than that.

On the conceptual level, Victor knew he could—perhaps should—revel in the downtime and find some way to amuse himself. He could catch up on his reading, or chat with the crews of the other Cataphracts, or even just go back to sleep.

But where was Lady Fenvale?

Victor stared upward and rolled the question around in his head. Logically, she was still in the manor house across the road. But it wasn't like her to sleep in—it wasn't like her to stay still. Victor supposed she might find some other means of occupying herself: fencing drills, perhaps. Except it was already late in the morning, and she still hadn't checked in on her dog or her Cataphract. Not to mention the fact she'd promised to bring table scraps for Lily.

Which left Victor mulling over the very real possibility that Lady Fenvale had been detained or waylaid somehow. But if she had, why hadn't anyone come for him? The *Huntress* was both dangerous and valuable, so any scheme against Lady Fenvale would have to secure it to have any chance of success. Or had the plan not got that far yet? Had Victor somehow thrown a wrench into the conspirators' scheme when he declined to attend the banquet and spent the night with the *Huntress* instead?

Victor shook his head and told himself he was probably just being paranoid.

Probably.

"I'm sure everything's fine, Lily," Victor said as he climbed out of the hammock. At the mention of her name, the big dog canted her head to the side, puzzled. "But perhaps we should go check on Lady Fenvale. She'll be glad to see you, don't you think?"

Lily's tongue darted out to wash over her black nose.

"I'll take that as a yes." He nodded and set off towards Duchess Rosalind's manor house, Lily following close behind. It was a short walk across the Cataphract road, but Victor couldn't help but feel exposed as he crossed the stretch of hard, level stone. Still, nobody from the big house cared to raise any objection; in fact, no one from the big house made much sound at all. It was even sleepier and quieter than the camp on the other side of the road.

The front door was unlocked.

Upon first walking into the manor house, Victor thought he'd somehow stumbled into an art gallery. He couldn't see the color of the wood paneling, as row after row of portraits and landscapes lined the walls. Hardwood tables and chairs were set up in the corners of the room, and Lily wasted little time in sniffing about for any scraps that might have been left over from the night before.

"Lily." Victor snapped his fingers to get the mastiff's attention away from the scavenger's buffet waiting for her. "You can eat as much as you like once we find Lady Fenvale."

The dog huffed in mild annoyance. Victor wasn't sure how much the mastiff understood (or how much she actually listened to him), but she still stepped away from the table before she could knock it over. Lily licked a few crumbs from her lips, then tilted her nose up in the air. Her nostrils twitched, and soon the big dog padded deeper into the manor house. Victor didn't know if Lily was tracking down her mistress or heading for the kitchen, but he followed anyway.

Every so often a maid or footman would hurry by, paying no attention to the rumpled man or the big dog prowling through the house; the staff had other things to worry about. They passed by open doorways leading to rooms full of snoring officers and aristocrats, laid out upon couches or piles of cushions. And those were the normal results of a night's debauchery. In one room, a quartet of marble statues had been arrayed around a round table, with hands of cards jokingly laid out in front of them. Someone had even put their wide-brimmed hat upon a bust of King Leopold the Brilliant. In another room, a large white goose took up a defensive position upon the back of a couch, splaying its wings out and hissing at anyone who dared to get too close.

Even Lily avoided that one.

Their meandering path took them up a floor and to the far end of one wing. Lily stopped in front of a pair of double doors and pawed at them, her claws scratching the light pink paint.

"Is she in here?" Victor asked the dog—only to get a plaintive whine in response. Victor took that as an affirmative, then cleared his throat before knocking smartly on the door. "Er—Lady Fenvale? Are you in there?"

"Who's that?" The voice, though muffled through the door, was unmistakably Lady Fenvale's.

Victor wasn't the only one to recognize it, either. At the sound of her mistress' voice, Lily's floppy ears perked forward. The big dog lowered her head and pushed against the light doors, putting her not-inconsiderable bulk into it. While the latch was closed, it wasn't meant to hold up against over two hundred pounds of monster-hunting hound, and the soft wood splintered around the lock as the doors swung inward. Lily rushed through into a lavishly furnished bedroom. Victor followed—and immediately wished he hadn't.

Startled by the sudden noise, Lady Fenvale sprang out of the large canopy bed on the other side of the room. She yanked her saber from where her scabbard hung on the bedpost, ready to meet her attacker with naked steel—and naked everything else. Sword in hand, dark hair mussed and wild, Lady Fenvale looked like nothing so much as a vengeful warrior goddess from some ancient legend. At least she did until she recognized the source of the commotion, and her expression slumped into one of confusion. "Lily?" She lowered her sword, only to raise it back up again as she registered who else was in the room. "Victor?"

With his face burning hot from embarrassment, Victor immediately turned his back on Lady Fenvale. He'd only had a fleeting, inadvertent glimpse of brown skin and long limbs, but it was certainly more than he'd ever intended to see.

"Lily!" Behind Victor, from the direction of the bed, a second woman spoke. "Who's a good girl?" Lily let out a happy canine grunt, and the unknown woman giggled.

Victor slowly, silently crept towards the door—only to freeze as Lady Fenvale's voice spoke again.

"Stop."

Victor prepared to die. At least with his back turned, he wouldn't see it coming. He would at least have the luxury of a quick death; Lady Fenvale was merciful— and efficient. Victor figured she could chop his head off with a single stroke, and then he'd be free of embarrassment.

"Wait outside, Victor. I'll be right out." Metal slid over metal as Lady Fenvale slid her sword back into its scabbard, and not into Victor's neck. "And close the door."

The other woman giggled again.

"Of course." Between the broken latch and his own ardent refusal to turn around, shutting the double doors proved something of an awkward process. He stood guard in the hallway, protecting what was left of Lady Fenvale's dignity—and the safety of anyone who might blunder in after him. On the other side of the door, Lady Fenvale had a quick hushed conversation with the other woman, but the two kept their voices low enough so Victor couldn't distinguish exactly what they said. Thankfully, everyone else in the house was either asleep or too busy to pay them any attention.

Minutes later, Lady Fenvale opened the doors and stepped into the hallway with Lily at her side. She'd got her clothes back on and tied her dark hair back into a loose ponytail. Once the bedroom doors closed, Lady Fenvale and Victor said the same thing, at the same time:

"I can explain."

"You don't need to." Victor spoke quickly, before Lady Fenvale could tell him to shut up. "Er, explain, that is. I was out of line. I never should have come looking for you. It's just that the morning was getting late, and after everything else I was afraid that this was some convoluted plot of your cousin's, so I brought Lily to make sure you hadn't been captured or jailed, which you obviously hadn't been, and I should have known that once your dog led me up to the second floor, but then she just pushed the door in before I could stop her, and—"

"Victor." Lady Fenvale's voice was stern, but not angry. "Breathe."

"Trying to," Victor wheezed.

"Good. Now shut up."

"Trying to do that, too."

"It's my fault for sleeping until—what time is it, anyway?"

"Almost midday, I think," Victor said.

"That late? Damn." Lady Fenvale rubbed at the bridge of her nose. "I never should have let Sophia—er—Lady Rosalind—the Duchess' daughter—"

"Your friend," Victor added, in hopes of making the conversation less awkward, or at least shorter.

"Yes, my—"

"Your what?" Behind them, the doors opened, and Lady Sophia Rosalind stepped out. She was a vision of chestnut hair and porcelain skin, wrapped in a dark, fur-lined robe. The robe was too large for Lady Rosalind's slim frame, and the collar hung open to reveal the scandalous bare curve of her shoulder. Lady Rosalind paid little attention to Victor, instead smiling up at Lady Fenvale with mischief in her green eyes.

Lady Fenvale cleared her throat. "My ... close friend."

"Mm. That will have to do." Lady Rosalind giggled again, then stood up on tiptoe to kiss Lady Fenvale on the cheek. "You shouldn't be in such a hurry to leave, Diana. You forgot something."

"I did?"

Lady Rosalind just laughed, then brought her other hand out from behind her back, holding Lady Fenvale's saber and sword belt. Upon seeing the weapon, Lady Fenvale reached for her left hip, confirming her unarmed state. Victor, meanwhile, astutely did not speculate about the sort of distraction that could make Lady Fenvale forget her sword. Lady Rosalind pressed the weapon into Lady Fenvale's hands and smiled. "I'll leave you to your business, Diana. But don't leave too soon, mm? I still haven't seen what your *Huntress* can do."

Lady Rosalind winked and withdrew, closing the double doors behind her. Lady Fenvale took a deep breath, then busied herself with buckling her sword back on before she set off down the hallway with Victor and Lily in tow. As they walked out of the house, some of the party guests began to wake up and stumble about, which only added to the genteel chaos and gave Lady Fenvale an opening to escape unnoticed, even with a massive dog and an anxious engineer accompanying her.

She remained quiet until they made it out the front door and halfway across the Cataphract road.

"I trust you, Victor," Lady Fenvale said, keeping her voice low. "Which is why I know you will remain silent as to what you just saw."

"Right." Victor nodded. "I won't. Er—tell anyone, that is. Not that there's anything to tell. It's like you said, you and Lady Rosalind are friends. Close friends. And I'm sure, given the number of guests the Rosalinds are, er, entertaining, it makes perfect sense that Lady Rosalind, being a gracious host, let you sleep in her—er, I think I'll just stop talking now."

"Thank you, Victor," Lady Fenvale said. "I ... I trust you shall remain discreet over the next few days, given that Duchess Rosalind has asked us to stay for a short while."

"But I thought we had to make it to the capital as soon as we could?"

"That was my original plan, yes. But we can spare half a week or so, given we've at least been acknowledged with a formal escort. So long as Kingsforge knows I'm on my way with the *Huntress* to take the Cataphract Oath, my cousin won't be able to lay claim to what's rightfully mine. So we can rest—if just for a few days. It'll be nice to enjoy some peace and quiet, don't you think, Victor?"

Victor looked over his shoulder at Duchess Rosalind's house, just in time to see a white goose waddle through the open front doors.

"Peace and quiet. Right," he said.

CHAPTER 4

The *Huntress* lunged.

The point of her sword drove towards the center of the *Mad Tiger*'s torso, but the other duelist pushed the attack aside with the haft of her poleaxe. The *Mad Tiger* planted her feet and swiveled at the waist, her entire torso spinning in a complete circle to add more force to her counterattack. A half-ton of gleaming war steel swung towards the *Huntress*' visor, only barely stopped from striking its target by a last-minute parry.

Ratcheted gears in the *Mad Tiger*'s waist clicked, and soon the Cataphract's torso whirled around in the opposite direction, attacking the *Huntress* from the opposite side. Unable to get her broadsword around in time, the *Huntress* could only twist around and lower her shoulder to catch the blow on the thick metal of her shoulder armor. The axe hit with a hellacious clang, leaving a couch-length dent smashed deep into the unpainted metal. Still, the armor did its job, protecting the vulnerable joint beneath.

Before the *Mad Tiger* could cycle around for a third swing, the *Huntress* sprang into action. Her blade skidded against the *Mad Tiger*'s poleaxe, steel scraping on steel until the broadsword's crossguard locked with the haft of her opponent's weapon. In so close, the *Huntress* didn't have the room to swing her heavy sword, but the tangled weapons kept the *Mad Tiger* from repeating her whirling attack. And so, the battle came down to a shoving match, a test of pure mechanical power. Metal joints and plating groaned under the strain, but the two duelist-class Cataphracts were evenly matched, neither able to overwhelm the other. The *Mad Tiger* fell back a step, then braced its foot against the grassy ground to shove back against the *Huntress* even harder.

Blue smoke poured from each Cataphract's vents as they grappled, each machine's alchemical furnace pumping out as much power as possible. The *Huntress'* feet dug twin furrows through the ground as she was steadily forced backward—until the blue of her exhaust fumes grew thicker and darker, pulsing steadily like the wheezing of some great beast. With a renewed strength, Lady Fenvale's Cataphract surged forward and grabbed the haft of her opponent's poleaxe with her left hand. With a heave and a yank, the *Huntress* ripped the weapon out of the *Mad Tiger's* grasp, one-handed. The *Mad Tiger* staggered, off-balance, and the *Huntress* followed through with a smashing pommel blow to the other Cataphract's shoulder.

The *Mad Tiger* fell to one knee and lurched to the side. With a turn of her wrist, the *Huntress* touched the edge of her broadsword against the bottom rim of the *Mad Tiger's* visor, ready to lever the metal cowling open. She held her stolen poleaxe with her other hand, parallel with the ground and off to one side, ready to fend off any Cataphract that might try to come to the rescue. All it would take was a simple shift of the *Huntress'* blade to force open the *Mad Tiger's* visor and reveal her vulnerable captain within. The *Mad Tiger* was at the *Huntress'* mercy, and both captains knew it.

The Cataphracts froze.

After a long, silent minute, the defeated Cataphract opened her visor. The *Mad Tiger's* captain stood up in his helm-seat. The young man paid no attention to the enormous blade precariously close, instead keeping his eyes on the *Huntress'* still-closed visor. He pulled his wide-brimmed hat from his head and bowed. "Well done, Lady Fenvale!"

The crowd cheered.

Duchess Rosalind clapped her gloved hands politely, and the other nobles and officers seated around her followed suit. The "training exercise" had made for great entertainment; Victor supposed it was at least better than another of Carondel's plays. The Duchess' daughter, Lady Sophia Rosalind, watched the bout with particular interest and waved a lacy blue handkerchief in the air as she cheered.

Victor wondered if Lady Fenvale had a matching one tucked into her doublet.

Victor didn't dwell on the thought, as he was soon distracted by the rest of the squadron's engineers. There was a great deal of good-natured jostling and backslapping as various bets were settled. Victor smiled graciously as the *Mad Tiger*'s crew chief pushed a handful of silver coins into his palm. He'd made the bet mostly on principle, out of confidence in his work (not to mention Lady Fenvale's skill), but Victor had kept the wager small enough that winning or losing wouldn't hurt too badly.

"It was a close thing." Victor pocketed his meager winnings and nodded to the *Mad Tiger*'s grizzled crew chief. "That trick with the waist swivel, I've never seen a Cataphract move like that. How do you keep the control cables from getting twisted and tangled?"

"Special design, unique to the *Mad Tiger*. Something of a secret," the man said. "But how'd you manage to get so much power out of the *Huntress*? Takes most duelists both hands to lift something as heavy as the *Mad Tiger*'s axe. Your *Huntress* swung it around like it was nothing."

"It's, er, something of a secret?" Victor pocketed his winnings.

"Hah! That's it. If Her Ladyship ever cuts you loose, send me a letter. The *Mad Tiger* could use a smart lad like you."

"I'll keep that in mind, thank you. But if you'll excuse me, I'd better go check in on the *Huntress*." Victor bid his polite farewell and headed back to where the *Huntress* knelt. By the time he got there, Lady Fenvale had descended from her Cataphract's helm, landing on the ground with a victorious bounce in her step. Lily was the first to congratulate her on her victory, wagging her tail happily as she trotted over.

Proud, Lady Fenvale patted the massive foot of the *Huntress*. "She's fighting well."

"I'm glad to hear that." Victor looked up at the Cataphract. The size of the fresh dent in the *Huntress*' unpainted pauldron made him wince. "But, ah—how many of these 'training exercises' do you have planned? Because if something were to happen and you damaged the *Huntress'* motive gears, or even her alchemical furnace, I don't know what we'd do for a replacement. Or, well, I do know what we could do for a replacement, but it would be … inconvenient to try a repeat of what happened at Maldrinne Manor."

"A fair point." Lady Fenvale nodded. "But don't worry. Now that the other captains have seen what the *Huntress* is capable of, I doubt many of them will be too eager to face—"

"Diana!" Lady Rosalind bustled over, her fancy parasol bobbing with each step. The other engineers and crewmen hurried out of her way, making room for the Duchess' daughter and the small platoon of handmaidens and servants trailing behind her. Lady Rosalind ignored well-dressed staff and grease-spattered crewmen alike, focusing completely on Lady Fenvale. "That was glorious! Like something out of one of the old legends!"

"I don't know if I'd go that far," Lady Fenvale said, voice softer and friendlier than Victor had ever heard before. "But thank you, nonetheless."

"You don't have to play humble." Lady Rosalind stepped in close enough to bat at Lady Fenvale's arm. "You're magnificent, and you shouldn't try to pretend otherwise."

"I'll keep that in mind," said Lady Fenvale.

"You'd better." Lady Rosalind giggled and patted Lady Fenvale's arm again. It was a small, subtle gesture, but still enough to make Victor glance away. He looked over at Lady Rosalind's gaggle of staff instead, and found them likewise studiously ignoring their mistress chatting away with the *Huntress'* captain. He wondered how much they knew about Lady Rosalind's history with Lady Fenvale— more than he did, probably. Then again, that wasn't a high bar to clear.

Lady Rosalind prattled on. "I do hope all this fighting has stoked your appetite, Diana—I've had the staff prepare the most decadent lunch. You still like those little almond cakes, don't you?"

"If they're even half as good as I remember." Lady Fenvale nodded. "But please, allow me a few minutes to clean up. I'd rather not dine while still smelling of alchemical smoke."

Lady Rosalind leaned forward and made a show of sniffing the air around Lady Fenvale. "You smell fine to me."

"I'm not sure your other guests will think the same thing."

"We could dine in private. You could have all the cakes."

"I'd make myself sick."

"Oh, fine. You win." Lady Rosalind affected a melodramatic pout and patted Lady Fenvale on the arm again. "But don't keep me waiting, hm?" She gave her parasol a little twirl, then turned to head back to the manor house, her staff and handmaidens obediently following along.

Victor cleared his throat and seized on the one thing he had any business commenting on. "You, ah—you're not smelling smoke in the helm-seat, are you? If you are, that would indicate a leak, even though the exhaust vents have been—"

"It's fine, Victor," Lady Fenvale said. "There aren't any leaks. I just needed to ... " She trailed off and looked down at her rumpled, sweaty doublet. "I've got fresh clothes in my luggage. I think. But if you're really concerned about the exhaust, run whatever tests you need to."

"It'll take the better part of a day," Victor said.

"That's fine. Duchess Rosalind has asked General Barrowgale and the other officers to go riding with her tomorrow. I might bring Lily. She'd enjoy the exercise." Lady Rosalind said, albeit without much enthusiasm, enough of a change that even Victor could notice.

"Is ... something wrong, Lady Fenvale?" he asked.

"Last night, Sophia— Lady Rosalind offered me a ... possibility."

"She did?"

"The Rosalinds have not had a Cataphract to their name for years. But if I pledge myself, pledge the *Huntress* to the Rosalinds—" Lady Fenvale looked up at her Cataphract, armor gleaming in the morning sun. "It'd give the family quite a bit more social clout than they currently have. And it'd mean that I could stay. That we could stay. Duchess Rosalind is known for her hospitality, after all."

"Ah."

"You'd still have a place with the *Huntress*, of course." Lady Fenvale added on. "You've done wonders getting her operational again, and I can't think of any other alchemical engineers I'd trust with her continued maintenance. I'm sure the Rosalinds would be happy to provide you with a workshop and materials to do so. And if you needed help, I imagine it wouldn't be hard to enlist Master-Smith Chalment's assistance, either."

"That's certainly an appealing prospect," said Victor. "Marissa, which is to say, Master-Smith Chalment is an exceptionally talented craftswoman, and she would no doubt be an asset. Due to her, er, talents. Leaving aside any personal feelings I might have on the matter, which are honestly irrelevant in the grander scheme of things —"

"You don't need to explain yourself, Victor." Lady Fenvale pursed her lips, then looked back in the direction of Rosalind Manor. "And neither do I."

"So it's settled, then?" Victor said.

"Not yet, no." Lady Fenvale shook her head. "As there's at least one … complication."

"Which is?"

"If I pledge the *Huntress*, pledge myself to the Rosalind family, I won't be able to swear the Cataphract Oath to the crown, and my father's lands and titles will fall to my cousin."

"Ah." Victor mulled the situation over. "But we've still got the *Guilt of Gold*'s alchemical furnace. Surely, that offers us leverage? Perhaps we could arrange some sort of trade."

"That's not the issue, Victor. It's not just a matter of my bastard cousin's schemes, it's a matter of law. The Fenvale's lands and titles were chartered by the crown, and therefore only the King himself can renew them. If I become a vassal to the Rosalind family, I'll renounce all of that." Lady Fenvale clutched her left hand into a fist over her saber's pommel. "Which means my cousin wins. And not from anything he did, but from a decision that I made myself. I can already hear him gloating."

"You've not made your decision yet." Victor furrowed his brow. "Have you?"

"No," said Lady Fenvale. "Not yet."

"Ah, good." Victor said. "As, well, my own opinions on such a weighty matter shouldn't influence you in the slightest. You've hired me to maintain the *Huntress*, and I can do that here, or at Kingsforge, or wherever we may wind up. Though having Master-Smith Chalment's … assistance would by no means be unpleasant, the very last thing I want is for you to take it into any sort of consideration. I've known you long enough to trust your judgement, Lady Fenvale. All I ask is that you take as much time as you need to make the right decision."

"Thank you, Victor." Lady Fenvale trailed off into silence, again reaching down to stroke a hand down Lily's back, causing the hackleback mastiff to let out a happy grunt. A few moments passed.

"Then it's settled." Lady Fenvale nodded. "We'll depart for Kingsforge tomorrow."

"Oh." Victor blinked. "I guess the decision was easier than I thought?"

"Easy, nothing. You don't have to tell Lady Rosalind."

Lady Fenvale did not spend the evening in Rosalind Manor, as she had the several nights prior. Instead, she slept at the *Huntress'* helm-seat, as she'd done on the road. As the morning sun rose, so did Lady Fenvale.

"When can we march?" Lady Fenvale asked the question as she clambered down the rope ladder dangling from her Cataphract's helm-seat.

At the time, Victor briefly considered asking Lady Fenvale how the conversation with Lady Rosalind went, but prudently thought the better of it. With the sun rising, Victor's opinion remained the same, so he seized on a safer subject instead.

"Any time you wish." Victor nodded as he fastened his boots. He'd gotten used to waking up before dawn, even while enjoying the Rosalind's hospitality. "Though I can't say the same for the rest of the squadron. Given they're supposed to be our honor guard, leaving without General Barrowgale and company may come off as a little ... impolite." Victor paused as a thought struck him, then pushed his glasses further up his nose as he stood up. "General Barrowgale *does* know you mean to leave today, yes?"

"I made him aware of my intentions last night, yes. And he said he'd be happy to accompany us to the capital ... at *his* pace." Lady Fenvale surveyed the dormant camp, barely lit by the first rays of a still-red sunrise. She tapped an impatient finger against the pommel of her saber, peering expectantly eastward, as if an annoyed glare were enough to make the sun rise faster.

Lily, meanwhile, slowly got up from where she'd been curled up in the shadow of the *Huntress'* left heel, gave a canine stretch, and then trotted over to lean against Lady Fenvale's side, tail wagging lazily. The canine gesture immediately improved Lady Fenvale's mood, as she reached down to scratch at the big dog's ears.

"And good morning to you too," she said, then turned her attention back to Victor. "I think I'd better stretch my legs before we get underway. Maybe find some breakfast for Lily. That should give General Barrowgale time enough to get *King Leopold's Pardon* ready to march, don't you think?"

"I admire your optimism, Lady Fenvale."

"You might be the first person to ever call me an optimist." Lady Fenvale smiled as she said it. She clapped Victor on the shoulder, not hard enough to make him stagger, but close. "We'll be

31

back before long. Make sure there's nothing else you need to attend to, as we'll be leaving as soon as we can."

Victor nodded. "Of course."

With that, Lady Fenvale strode off, Lily following close beside her.

As the sun climbed higher above the eastern horizon, the crews of the other Cataphracts in the squadron began to wake, and set about preparing their own machines for the coming journey. Having already double and triple-checked the *Huntress* the night before, Victor found himself in the odd position of not having anything to do. He thought about offering assistance to the *King Leopold Pardon*'s crew, but decided against it. He'd likely just get in the way of the larger, more experienced crew. That, and he felt like he needed to stay with the *Huntress*, just in case Lady Fenvale returned unexpectedly.

Instead, Victor unwrapped a bit of leftover bread and sausage out of his bag for a light breakfast, grateful for the fact that Lady Fenvale had taken Lily with her, and therefore the big dog wouldn't try to beg any scraps from him. After finishing his breakfast, Victor took a sketchbook and a charcoal pencil from his bags, sat down on the *Huntress'* left foot, and started scribbling down a few notes on potential improvements he could make to the *Huntress* at some point in the future. Some of her armor plating would need replacing once they made it to Kingsforge, which Victor knew could be a prime opportunity for an upgrade. He spent several pleasant minutes scribbling out rough calculations, estimating just how heavy of a load the *Huntress'* frame could carry, as well as how much such an amount of steel might cost.

"Engineer Brinden?"

"Hm?" Victor looked up, then stood up as quickly as he could once he realized Lady Rosalind was, inexplicably, not just standing in front of the *Huntress*, but talking to *him,* of all people.

"Ah!" Victor turned about, startled. "Lady Rosalind. To, uh, what do I owe the honor?"

Even with the early hour, Lady Rosalind was impeccably attired in lace and ruffles so white that made Victor became immediately conscious of his charcoal-smudged hands. Just to be on the safe side, Victor took a half-step back, in case his mere proximity was enough to soil Lady Rosalind's dress.

"Diana isn't about." Lady Rosalind attempted a scowl, but her delicate features made the expression more of a pout. "Where is she?"

"Lady Fenvale went to stretch her legs for a bit before our departure."

"So you really are leaving, then?" Lady Rosalind's scowl-pout grew deeper. "And here I'd hoped Diana was bluffing. Still--" Lady Rosalind glided over to the *Huntress'* left toe, at which point she tapped a finger on the unyielding steel. "At least this is an opportunity to see what Diana loves more than-- more than anything."

"Oh." Victor wiped his hands on the edge of his leather apron in an attempt to clear the worst of the grime from them. "I wouldn't presume to guess Lady Fenvale's intentions--"

"But?" Lady Rosalind arched an eyebrow.

"But—" Victor gulped. "The *Huntress* has belonged to the Fenvales for generations, and as such, this Cataphract is both her birthright and her responsibility. Especially with the untimely passing of Count Fenvale."

"Especially with that." Lady Rosalind let out a heavy sigh, causing her myriad ruffles and ribbons to rise and fall.

"I'm sure you realize why this Cataphract-- why the Catapract Oath is so important to Lady Fenvale, then. And, as such, her departure to tend to such matters in no way reflects on her ... personal opinions."

"Hm." Lady Rosalind mused, skeptical. Again, she ran her fingertips over the white-enameled armor of the *Huntress'* ankle. "It is a ... complex thing, isn't it? A Cataphract, that is."

"Right again, Lady Rosalind." Victor said. " Each Cataphract is a unique work of craftsmanship, maintained and improved over years-- sometimes decades, sometimes even centuries. The *Huntress* is, in all honestly, a fascinatingly intricate machine, even compared to some of the other Cataphracts in the squadron. Which sounds like a boast, but I assure you it's only the truth. Why, if you were to measure the *Huntress'* hand articulation against that of the *Mad Tiger*--" Victor blinked, then cleared his throat as his reined in his impulsive enthusiasm. "But, ah, I'll not lecture you on the boring details."

"Don't worry yourself on my account. There's something to be said for listening to an expert, even if you haven't the faintest idea of what they're talking about. Still, I wonder." Lady Rosalind trailed her gloved fingertips across the *Huntress'* armored boot, "what if there were something wrong? Nothing catastrophic, but something that would delay your departure a for a day? Possibly two?'

"Impossible." Victor drew himself up taller and shook his head. "The *Huntress* is in the best condition she's ever been in. At least, leaving aside certain ... cosmetic blemishes to her armor that I simply haven't had the materials or facilities to repair yet. But her fundamental mechanisms are all in excellent condition, I've made sure of that."

"Of course they are." Lady Rosalind waved a hand, idly. "But what if you, perhaps, *found* some something requiring a delay?"

"That's highly unlikely."

Lady Rosalind turned to face Victor, then took a step closer. "Perhaps I could convince you to take another look?" She fluttered her eyelashes. Dangerously so.

It took Victor a moment to process the implication but once he did, his face paled and his stomach churned. "I-- I'm *sure* I have misunderstood you, Lady Rosalind. As, well, a lady of your standing surely would not deign to bribe, or blackmail, or so much as ... cajole a humble alchemical engineer such as myself. Not that I could be bribed or blackmailed or cajoled in the first place. In any matter, much less anything as important as the *Huntress'* continued and efficient operation." Victor backpedaled until he felt his back press up against the unyielding metal of the *Huntress'* right heel.

"Ha!" Lady Rosalind tittered a laugh, then held a hand up to her mouth. "Oh, you are either terribly naive, or terribly polite."

"Likely both, to be honest."

"Indeed." Lady Rosalind giggled again. "I suppose I should have known better. Diana values loyalty, and she inspires it. She must trust you a great deal, now that you've gotten her favorite toy working again."

Victor sputtered. "The *Huntress* is not a--"

Lady Rosalind rolled her eyes. "And now you're starting to *sound* like her."

Victor blinked. "I am?"

"Not verbatim, but close enough. Whenever Diana starts going on about this ... machine, she gets the same look in her eye. That same ... fervent tone of voice. Perhaps that just means you and the Lady you serve share the same sort of madness." Lady Rosalind looked up at the *Huntress* again, suspicious. "So, do what you must, and prepare your machine for whatever terrible adventure Lady Fenvale is going to throw herself into. But, I would ask just one favor."

"And that is?"

"Take care of her."

"That, er, that is my job."

"I meant Lady Fenvale, not the *Huntress*."

"So did I," said Victor. "Though, er, to be honest, the two are somewhat intertwined."

"That they are." Lady Rosalind smiled a sad smile. "And that's the problem, isn't it?"

By the time Lady Fenvale returned to the *Huntress*, Lady Rosalind had already left. She he could still be seen walking across the Cataphract road, back to Rosalind House, a puff of pale ribbonry and lace receding into the distance. Close enough that Lady Fenvale could have gotten her attention, if she shouted, or catch up to her if she hurried.

She did not.

Lady Fenvale stood still long enough to watch Lady Rosalind disappear through the front doors of the manor house, but made no move to call out or follow her. Once Lady Rosalind was out of view, Lady Fenvale turned her attention to Victor.

"I've spoken with General Barrowgale-- we shall depart within the hour. Perhaps earlier, if we're lucky." She reached for the rope ladder that led up to the *Huntress*' helm-seat, then paused. "What did Lady Rosalind want?"

"She-- she wants you to stay." Victor fidgeted with his sketches and calculations. "Quite ardently."

"As I'm aware." Lady Fenvale tightened her fingers around a rung of the rope ladder. "I suppose she asked you to convince me to stay a while longer."

"In a manner of speaking, yes."

"And?" Lady Fenvale arched a brow. Dangerously so.

"And I, er, declined. Firmly but politely." Victor said. "After all, I've known you long enough to know that, once you've set your mind to something, there's no force in the world that could make you stray from your chosen path."

"Sophia's known me far longer than you have. You'd think she would've come to the same conclusion."

"I do not know Lady Rosalind well enough to make any sort of definitive judgement, but perhaps she's got the same sense of ... conviction that you do?"

"Stubborness, you mean."

36

"Putting it impolitely, yes?" Victor said as diplomatically as he could manage. "Although, if we were to look at it from another angle, that Lady Rosalind would go to such lengths to keep you here is something of an indication of her ... inclinations. If not intentions. Towards you, that is. Which is to say--"

"Victor?"

"Yes?"

"Stop talking."

"Thank you," Victor said with no small degree of relief.

"The fact of the matter is," Lady Fenvale spoke as she climbed the rope ladder leading to the *Huntress'* helm-seat. "Lady Rosalind's inclinations, whatever they may be, are of no importance. As are my own. All that matters is that we take the *Huntress* to Kingsforge, where I shall swear the Cataphract Oath. So now, we march."

This said, Lady Fenvale closed the *Huntress'* visor. The white-armored cataphract rumbled as she stood, and blue smoke puffed from her vents as she took a long, ponderous step towards the Cataphract road.

Towards Kingsforge.

CHAPTER 5

Part city, part factory, part fortress, Kingsforge was the oldest, grandest city in the entire world. Centuries ago, the valley had contained the whole of civilization—the whole of humanity. The jagged, snowcapped peaks of the Lastwalls kept out roaming, ravenous Behemoths—and offered mankind the means to fight back. The ring of mountains were rich in the ore and lumber needed to build the first Cataphracts—as well as the means to power them. Deep underground, in a secret location only known to the royal family and their most loyal retainers, sat the Kingsforge itself, the mysterious cavern from which the city took its name. There, deep underground, the first of the Cataphract Kings discovered the miracle of the alchemical furnace.

In the generations since the first Cataphracts set out to reclaim the world, Kingsforge grew from a nameless redoubt into the gilded heart of Leovaix. The city expanded from one end of the valley to the other, then grew upwards once buildings started butting up against the Lastwalls. Towers of gray granite, buttressed by ornately carved arches, stretched up into the air, but they were still dwarfed by the Lastwalls themselves. Even with the sea of buildings crammed up against each other, there were still wide Cataphract roads laid out through the city, allowing even enormous siegebreakers to traverse the city.

At the heart of the city (and therefore, at the heart of the kingdom) was the Steel Circle, a round plaza paved with the same alchemically treated stone of the Cataphract roads. The Foundry-Palace of the Cataphract Kings sat on the far end of the circle, guarded by two enormous, ancient siegebreakers: the Inevitability and the Tribute. The Cataphracts stood on either side of a village-sized balcony, from which King Willem the Twelfth and his closest advisors could survey the plaza from four stories up. In faint imitation of the Lastwalls looming in the distance, tall walls of square-cut stone ran along the edge of the circle, capped with green, manicured gardens instead of ice. Hundreds of banners hung on the inside of the wall, crowded together to the point of overlapping. Each long banner bore a Cataphract's sigil. There was the shattered blade of the *Swordbreaker*, the lightning bolt of the *Peal of Thunder*, the burning flame of the famed siegebreaker *Conflagration*, and dozens more. Even the *Huntress'* leaping hound was on display, though the maroon and gold thread of her banner had faded with age.

Victor climbed up a steep staircase leading to the wall gardens, hoping he didn't look too out of place among the other spectators not royal enough to warrant space on the palace balcony. Since they'd arrived in Kingsforge, he had barely had enough time to change into more formal (or at least less rumpled) clothing and rush through the city ahead of the squadron so he could watch the oath ceremony. Were it not for the wide Cataphract roads cutting through the otherwise tightly packed city that led directly to the Steel Circle, Victor would have gotten lost, and even then it was a close thing.

Victor nervously tugged at the sleeves of his doublet, then made his way over to the edge of the wall garden, where a small crowd had gathered to watch General Barrowgale's squadron march in. A long table not too far from the stairwell was piled with refreshments. Victor got himself a glass of cool white wine and found himself glad he'd left Lily with some friendly engineers from the *Mad Tiger's* crew. The big dog would have ransacked the buffet as soon as everyone had their backs turned.

A trumpet blared to announce the Cataphracts' arrival. They marched in easy formation, two abreast—save for *King Leopold's Pardon*, which brought up the rear of the column on her own. As they entered the plaza, the *Bearbaiter* and the *Mad Tiger* veered off to the left, the *Kestrel* and the *Swordbreaker* to the right, each pair of Cataphracts taking up positions along the edge of the circle, while the *Huntress* marched straight forward, to the very center. *King Leopold's Pardon* brought up the rear of the formation and stopped as soon as she entered the circle, neatly blocking the way they came in.

At the center of the circle, before the king's gilded balcony, the *Huntress* planted the tip of her sword against the ground and descended into a kneel. In the shadow of the mountains, the palace, and the siegebreakers, the battered, white-armored duelist looked far smaller than she ever had before. The *Huntress'* visor eased open, revealing Lady Fenvale, clad in a pristine maroon coat with a leaping hound sigil stitched into the breast. She bowed at the waist and waited to be acknowledged.

"Who approaches the throne?" someone up on the balcony called out. Not King Willem himself, of course. Being a king meant having a whole regiment of people to shout on his behalf.

"I am Countess Diana Fenvale, captain of the *Huntress*." She raised her head and spoke with clear, chilling confidence that left no doubt as to her dedication. "I have come to pledge my service—and my Cataphract—to the service of the crown and the kingdom. May my sword be his, and his enemies be mine."

Silence.

Victor squinted up at the throne balcony and wished he'd brought a spyglass. At this distance, he could only see the throne itself, a gilded, high-backed monument that just happened to be in the vague shape of a chair. The king leaned over to mutter something to one of his courtiers, who passed the message along a few more steps down the chain until the king's herald spoke again.

"Let it be known that His Brilliance, King Willem the Twelfth, undefeated in battle, unparalleled in grace, protector of Leovaix, master of all alchemies, heir to the Cataphract Throne, he who is to be exalted beyond all others—" The listing of titles and honors went on for some minutes longer, to the point where Victor wondered if it were a test of Lady Fenvale's patience and stamina. Finally, the herald got on with the rest of the proclamation. "—does hereby accept Countess Fenvale's honorable and binding oath! General Barrowgale shall escort her, and her machine, the *Huntress*, to the Royal Arsenal, where she shall await further instruction and the appointment of her holdings."

Polite applause rippled through the crowd on the walls.

"Thank you, my king." Lady—no, Countess—Fenvale lowered herself back into the *Huntress'* helm, stood the machine up, and slowly turned to walk out of the Steel Circle, escorted by the *Bearbaiter* and the *Mad Tiger* and the rest. *King Leopold's Pardon*

40

stepped out of their way to let the squadron pass, then turned to follow them into the city proper. Once the Cataphracts disappeared from sight, the crowd in the gardens idly dispersed to whatever other games and gossip they had to entertain them.

"That's it?" Victor blurted.

"King Willem is a busy, busy man," a familiar voice— Marissa's voice—chimed in. "And since the *Stalwart* came in two days ago, there's not as much novelty in the full rigmarole."

"Marissa!" Victor smiled as he said the name. "Or, er— Master Smith Chalment. What a pleasant surprise."

"I can say the same. When I saw that bastard Dunsall bring the *Stalwart* in before you got here, I started to worry." Marissa neatly hooked her elbow in Victor's and guided him down the wall-top garden, away from the prying ears of other guests.

"How did he even manage that, anyway? The *Stalwart* was in pieces when we left."

"Which is why he was able to get ahead of you. Maldrinne loaded the *Stalwart* up on boats and shipped her down the Warden River, faster than a Cataphract could march."

"That's … rather clever. Risky, but clever." Victor ran over the scenario in his mind. "The *Stalwart*'s too big to move on a single barge—not safely, at least. But since she was already broken down into her component parts, each boat could just take an arm or a leg. But how did Dunsall get the *Stalwart* put back together again, now that you and he are on, ah … bad terms?" Victor paused. "You two are still on bad terms, aren't you?"

"He tried to kill me, Victor." Marissa patted Victor on the arm. "I won't forget that. But Marquis Maldrinne has deep pockets, and there's no shortage of engineers to take his coin. They reassembled the *Stalwart* a few miles outside the city. Something of a slapdash job, if you ask me. They at least got her walking again, and after that the marquis pulled some strings to make sure Dunsall could swear the Cataphract Oath as soon as possible. At least half of the noble families of the kingdom owe Maldrinne money, including the king. So when he wants something done, it happens."

"I didn't know Dunsall could even operate a Cataphract."

"He trained on an armature, back at Maldrinne House. Not extensively, but enough to march the *Stalwart* from one end of the parade ground to the next," Marissa said.

"Maybe it's for the best?" Victor tried for optimism. "Lady— ah, Countess Fenvale isn't one for ceremony. All she wanted was to keep the *Huntress* out of her cousin's hands, and she's done so."

"But now that she's taken the Cataphract Oath, Countess Fenvale is at the king's beck and call," Marissa said. "The king will send someone to hash out the details with her before too long. In the meanwhile, at least you'll have access to the Royal Arsenal."

"I will?"

"Of course you will. Every Cataphract in service to the Crown has a right to be outfitted there. It shouldn't be too much trouble to get the *Huntress* tended to, especially since you already know somebody who works at the arsenal."

"I do?" Victor asked.

Marissa laughed and leaned up to kiss Victor on the cheek. Her lips left a warm spot on Victor's skin, made even warmer by the blush that followed. "For such a clever man, you can be remarkably stupid."

The Royal Arsenal mirrored Kingsforge in both its layout and its character. It was crowded, loud, and built to serve towering war machines. Looking down the long plaza paved with alchemically treated stone, Victor recognized the forges, the winches, the drop hammers, the cable winders, the drive lathes, and all the other complex tools and equipment needed to build and maintain Cataphracts.

A row of training armatures sat beneath a large canvas awning, allowing engineers to experiment with different control layouts in wood and rope before applying them to the steel and cable of a proper Cataphract. Scaffolding, several stories high, lined both sides of the plaza, with narrow rope bridges stretching across like laundry lines. Cataphracts in various states of repair stood amidst the scaffolds, crews clambering around them with familiar ease. At a glance, Victor counted seven siegebreakers, thirteen duelists, and no fewer than two dozen skirmishers: enough tonnage to conquer a kingdom, were they all operational. Some of the war machines were armed and polished for parade, while others had been stripped down to their pipes and cabling. Victor saw the *Stalwart* some distance down the plaza, but the recently reassembled duelist was too far away for Victor to assess her condition.

The *Huntress* stood in one of the closer alcoves, with a crowd of curious engineers and journeymen gathered around her ankles. The Arsenal's crewmen showed far more interest in the *Huntress*' arrival than King Willem and his courtiers did. Countess Fenvale had already climbed down from the *Huntress*' helm-seat and reunited with Lily, who had accompanied the *Mad Tiger*'s crew to the Royal Arsenal ahead of the main squadron. With the dog at her side, Countess Fenvale chatted with the various officers and foremen of the Arsenal. In her sigil-embroidered tunic, polished boots, plumed hat, and heavy swordbelt, Lady Fenvale looked every inch the Cataphract captain. As Marissa and Victor approached, she glanced over.

"And this is my chief engineer, Victor Brinden." She beckoned Victor over.

Which is when he realized just what he'd gotten into.

The aged, well-dressed master engineers of the Royal Arsenal were, by their station, some of the most brilliant minds in all the kingdom: each one easily the equal of any of his teachers at the university. Between the half-dozen men and women chatting with Lady Fenvale, there must have been over a century of combined engineering experience. And here he was, a mere journeyman who'd botched his thesis presentation, working on a Cataphract as famed as the *Huntress*. It was ridiculous, and only a matter of time before the assembled masters saw him for what he was and acted accordingly. Surely, Doctor Waldwin or High Chemist Licielli had sent them a letter telling the other masters just how incompetent he was. And even if they hadn't, Marquis Maldrinne certainly would have spread word of his failures—

"I'm impressed," a man with a long gray beard draped over his leather smith's apron said. Victor blinked, faintly registering that words had been spoken, even if he didn't believe them. The man kept talking. "Countess Fenvale tells me that you got the *Huntress* up and running, all by yourself."

"Er, yes?" Victor said, as it was the truth.

The bearded man looked over his shoulder, up at the *Huntress*. "Wasn't long ago that they said it couldn't be done."

"Victor," Countess Fenvale cut in, "this is Doctor Sullustrom. He knew my father."

"Doctor Sullustrom?" Victor got his mouth working. "You—you wrote *A Treatise on Alchemical Energy Exchange*."

"You've read my work! That explains it! Anyone smart enough to appreciate my brilliance, which is something of a rarity in this day and age, is bound for great things, yes, sir."

"I don't know if I'd go that far. I mean, er, I'd never consider myself, er, great—"

"Not yet!" Doctor Sullustrom smiled through the thicket of his beard. "Now, you should meet my colleagues. They're always on the lookout for new talent."

This said, Doctor Sullustrom herded Victor from one introduction to the next, showing Victor off to some of the most respected (and widely published) minds in the kingdom. There was Chief Clockworker Gaston (author of *The Argument for Standardized Gearing Ratios*), Arch-Metallurgist Mollendra (*On the Application of Steels*), Engraver-General Kirbin (*A Comprehensive Listing of Cataphract Heraldry*), and half a dozen more. Of course, the presence of Master-Smith Marissa Chalment was a particular highlight, even though she hadn't written any definitive treatises. Yet.

Once Victor had met a reference library's worth of scholars and engineers, the introductions continued as he met their assistants, journeymen, and apprentices. All that talking came to be thirsty work, so some enterprising soul rolled in a few casks of wine, at which point it was more or less time for the day's work to stop anyway.

With the wine flowing, introductions turned into conversations, and conversations turned into celebrations. While the king had offered only the most cursory of acknowledgments back at the Steel Circle, the men and women of the Royal Arsenal offered a far more enthusiastic (and far less formal) reception. They raised their cups and mugs in toast—to the king, to the *Huntress*, to Countess Fenvale, and even to Victor. Which was something of a first on Victor's part, as he'd never been noteworthy enough to have anyone (much less a gathering of the most brilliant minds in Leovaix) drink to his health. Over sloshing, ever-full cups of wine, those brilliant minds chatted with Victor, to his mild astonishment. They asked his opinions on Cataphract design, on painting, on opera, on horses—Victor wondered if the questions were some sort of a test, like his examinations at university, or if they genuinely wanted to hear what he had to say. Still, his answers elicited smiles and nods more often than not, which Victor supposed was a good sign. Lady Fenvale weathered the celebrations easily—either from her robust warrior's constitution, or by slipping drinks to Lily when no one was looking. Victor thought the former more likely, as the big dog didn't look any the worse for wear, either. About an hour or two into the celebrations, she pulled Victor aside.

"Enjoy yourself, Victor. You've earned it." Lady Fenvale clinked her copper mug against his. "General Barrowgale's invited me to dinner with the rest of his squadron's captains. I trust you'll be fine on your own?"

"More than fine, honestly," Victor said. "I was just discussing certain theories of Behemoth anatomy with Doctor Grantelle before she went to get some more wine. She's working on a book, you know. Her thesis postulates that, by studying the bones and tendon structure of a Behemoth, the same physio-anatomical principles could be applied to Cataphract construction. Which would require a complete Behemoth skeleton for the best results, but all that we have left after all these years are fragments and trophies—"

"You'll be fine." Lady Fenvale grinned and patted Victor on the shoulder. "Just don't debate too hard. I don't know how long the king is going to make us wait here until he figures out what to do with us, but we might as well make the best of our time and start refitting the *Huntress* first thing tomorrow."

"Right!" Victor gulped down his wine, and nodded, resolute. "First thing. Tomorrow. In the morning." He peered into his now-empty mug and furrowed his brow. "What time is it now?"

"Time for me to go. Good night, Victor. I'll see you in the morning." Lady Fenvale tipped the brim of her hat, then set off. She whistled a quick command for Lily to follow her, and the two soon disappeared in the rowdy crowd.

Victor went back to the drinks and debates.

By the time the sun set, the assembled engineers had emptied the wine casks and started setting off in smaller groups to the various taverns and wineshops of the city. Despite numerous invitations, Victor stayed at the Arsenal, with the *Huntress*—mostly because staggering through the cramped alleys of Kingsforge's side streets was something he was loath to try sober, much less after several hours of celebration. And so, he sat on the ground, leaning against the side of the *Huntress'* foot. Somewhere along the line, Marissa settled in beneath his left arm, and he didn't see any reason to ask her to move. Instead, he figured he'd ask something else.

"Is it always like this?" Victor asked.

Marissa blinked and looked up at him. "Like what?"

"All the wine and singing and such. Do they do it every time a Cataphract arrives? Is this what happened when Dunsall brought the *Stalwart* in?" Victor craned his neck, looking around.

"Psssh, no. He threw some money at a couple of broke engineers to get the *Stalwart* put back together—that's hardly anything worth celebrating. However, when a brilliant young engineer singlehandedly restores a famous Cataphract that was thought to be unsalvageable? You're interesting, Victor. Which is much more than can be said about a boor like Rochen Dunsall. Or, well, Baron Dusnall now. Bah."

"Where is he, anyway?" Victor looked around, in case the big swordsman (and newly minted Cataphract captain) was lurking in the shadows. To Victor's wine-muddled mind, it seemed a plausible scenario—thankfully, Dunsall didn't show.

"Probably off licking someone's boots—or making someone lick his," Marissa huffed. "He hasn't been back to the Arsenal since he dropped the *Stalwart* off."

"So we're not likely to run into him by accident, at least."

"You always were an optimist, Victor. It's endearing. But—" Marissa patted him on the chest, then sat up straight so she could look him in the eyes. "Promise me you'll be careful. You've gotten yourself into some complicated business. I don't want you getting hurt."

"I appreciate the concern." Victor shifted his shoulders, trying to get comfortable. "But honestly, the worst should be behind us now that Lady Fenvale's taken the Cataphract Oath. The *Huntress* is up and running, so there's no way for the Marquis Maldrinne to get his hands on her now. I imagine things should settle down before long."

"You really think that, don't you?" Marissa sighed. Smiled. "And you know what, Victor? You might even be right. But no matter how it goes, there's nothing either of us can do about it right now, or right here." She braced a hand on the *Huntress'* foot as she stood and brushed some dirt from her skirts. "It's late, but my sister's house isn't that far."

"Is it safe to go alone? " Victor struggled up to his feet, helped along by Marissa's strong grip beneath his arm. "I, er, could escort you. That is, if you wanted." A warm flush rose to Victor's cheeks. Just from all the wine, he lied to himself.

"Kingsforge is quite safe, even at this hour," Marissa said.

"Oh."

"But I'd love the company." Marissa hooked her arm in his. "Besides, you haven't lined up a place to stay yet, have you?"

"Not exactly." Victor nervously reached up and pushed his glasses further up his nose. "There was—is just so much going on that I hadn't thought that far ahead. I suppose I could just find some canvas and hang a hammock between the *Huntress'* ankles—I've done it before. It's rather comfortable, once you get used to it."

"That's one option. Or—" Marissa squeezed Victor's arm tighter and leaned up to murmur into his ear. Warm breath tickled along his earlobe, making his pulse race. "I could offer an alternative."

"I—" Victor worked to get the words out of his suddenly dry mouth. "I think I would like that."

CHAPTER 6

Objectively speaking, Marissa Chalment had the most comfortable bed in existence.

Victor stared up at the ceiling, thinking over the implications of it all. Technically, Marissa Chalment's sister owned the most comfortable bed in existence and had elected to put it in the guest room. Either way, it was a fitting choice given the fact that Marissa Chalment was the most beautiful woman in existence.

Objectively speaking.

Morning sunlight streamed in through the open window and across the bed. Marissa's golden curls blazed gloriously where the sun hit them, and Victor propped himself up on one elbow to admire the view. The mattress creaked beneath him, and Marissa mumbled something incoherent before she wriggled in closer to Victor, burying her face in his chest to hide from the glare of the sun. Thus shielded, Marissa dozed off again and soon began to snore.

Which, in Victor's expert opinion, was the most melodic snore to ever grace a man's ear.

Objectively speaking.

They'd slipped in through the back the night before, so Victor hadn't got a good look around at the rest of Marissa's sister's townhouse. While the small guest room wasn't lavishly furnished or decorated, Victor couldn't think of any place he'd rather be.

The building's thick stone walls muffled the sound of the city outside and reduced the world down to a single quiet, cozy chamber, occupied by the most beautiful woman who had ever lived, and the ridiculously lucky man she'd chosen to keep her company.

Victor let his eyes drift shut again and settled in to savor the sheer perfection of the morning—

Which was when someone kicked in the door.

No, not someone—something. Victor sat upright just in time to see the door swing inward as a hulking brown blur shouldered its way into the room. He fumbled his glasses from the nightstand, sliding them onto his face so he could get a better look. Marissa shouted something obscene and rolled off the side of the bed, tangled in the blankets. The brown creature crossed the room in a single bound, landing on the mattress hard enough to make the bed creak precariously. The beast stood over Victor—and then leaned down to drag a washcloth-sized pink tongue up the side of his face.

"Lily!" Lady Fenvale's voice made the big dog stop slobbering. The countess whistled sharply, at which point the hackleback mastiff jumped off the bed and trotted proudly to her mistress' side. Lady Fenvale froze when she saw Victor's shocked state of undress (though he was at least still kept semi-decent by the blankets bunched up around his waist). The countess cleared her throat and fixed her gaze on a point somewhere above Victor's head. "My apologies, Victor. I—"

The metallic hammer-click of a pistol echoed in the small bedroom.

"—thought the worst," Lady Fenvale said.

"And so did I." Marissa stood up on the other side of the bed, holding a stubby-barreled pistol with both hands. The intimidatingly large caliber of the weapon balanced out the fact that Marissa didn't have a stitch of clothing on. She didn't so much as blush as she glared at Lady Fenvale over the sights of the flintlock. "You could have knocked, Countess."

"And you could have told someone where you were headed." Lady Fenvale kept her expression stony in the face of Marissa's pistol, even as she tightened her fingers around the hilt of her saber. Lily, picking up on her mistress' cue, pulled her lips back and bared her teeth at Marissa, rumbling a low, warning growl.

"I was unaware Victor had a curfew." Marissa lowered the gun, but kept glaring.

Lady Fenvale's hand eased away from the saber at her side. "And I was unaware he had a—"

"Misunderstanding!" Victor said. In perhaps one of the bravest things he'd ever done, he sprang to his feet and put himself between the two well-armed women with nothing to protect him but a wool blanket wrapped around his waist.

"This is all just a silly misunderstanding. My fault, really. I'm sure we'll all laugh about it once we've put it behind us. In fact, I'm laughing about it right now. Ha. Ha." He forced an unconvincing chuckle. Still, neither the countess nor the master smith tried to kill the other, which he took as a good sign.

"I'll wait for you outside," Lady Fenvale said curtly. Her boots thumped against the hardwood floor as she stepped backwards, disappearing around the corner of the doorway. She snapped her fingers, and Lily followed.

Marissa uncocked her pistol and put it back into the nightstand drawer she'd drawn it from. "You're more popular than I thought, Victor."

"I don't know if I'd go that far."

"Well, last thing I need right now is to deal with a jealous—"

"That won't be a problem." Victor found the certainty of the statement comforting. "Now, have you seen my pants?"

They dressed as quickly as they could manage. Marissa had the luxury of a clean set of clothing, while Victor was left with his rumpled formal attire from the night before. As they left, Marissa took a moment to glare at the door Lily had smashed through. "Who builds a door out of pine? In Kingsforge? Bah. My sister should've known better."

"She, er, she won't be angry with us, will she? Your sister, that is," Victor said.

"She's probably still asleep on the top floor. So long as we don't set the house on fire, she won't care. And I imagine the staff started running the moment they saw that countess of yours."

"Lady Fenvale can be quite intimidating when she puts her mind to it, yes," Victor said. He followed Marissa to the street outside, where Lady Fenvale and Lily waited. The street buzzed with activity, but everyone running around on their morning errands gave the tall woman with a sword and a large dog a wide berth. Lady Fenvale looked up as Marissa and Victor emerged.

"I must apologize, Master Smith Chalment." Lady Fenvale took off her hat and held it in both hands, contrite. "When I couldn't find Victor at the arsenal this morning, I began to fear he had been … waylaid. So I set Lily on his trail. She gets … excitable when she's picked up a scent, which is why she barged in as she did. I should have kept better control of her, and for that, I beg your forgiveness."

"That thing's name is Lily?" Marissa looked down at the big dog, slightly uneasy. "And they say you don't have a sense of humor."

Lady Fenvale bristled. "This 'thing' is a hackleback mastiff, the smartest, bravest, most versatile dog known to man. Lily is a perfectly appropriate name for a hound of her pedigree."

"I'll take your word for it," Marissa noted dryly. "Personally, I prefer cats."

"That explains a lot," Lady Fenvale said.

Victor cleared his throat. "As … diverting as it can be to discuss who likes what sort of pet, I'm sure Lady Fenvale has more important business, otherwise she wouldn't have gone through all the trouble of tracking us down."

"Right." Lady Fenvale nodded and pulled an envelope out of her pocket. The royal seal, nearly as wide across as Victor's palm and stamped on the paper in yellow wax, was impossible to miss. "King Willem has summoned us, Victor. We're to report to the palace this afternoon."

"What for?" Victor chewed at the inside of his cheek.

"Presumably, to receive my commission and find out what the king wants to do with the *Huntress*. Or at least to discuss it," Lady Fenvale said.

"That was quick," Marissa said. "As far as I know, Dunsall hasn't gotten his commission yet."

"Maybe the king wanted to wait until the *Huntress* arrived? That way, he could get everything out of the way at the same time?" Victor said.

"Optimist." Marissa smiled ruefully as she said it.

"I wouldn't presume to say what King Willem has planned." Lady Fenvale planted her hat back onto her head. "All I know is that we shouldn't keep him waiting."

"In that case, don't let me keep you," Marissa said. "I know what it's like to get pulled away on short notice. Not to mention the fact that I should probably get back to the arsenal anyway. I've some projects that need checking on. Find me there once you're done, Victor." She closed strong fingers into the fabric of Victor's doublet and pulled him in for a quick but no less thorough kiss.

"Mmmph," mmmph'd Victor.

Lady Fenvale just watched with an arched eyebrow, while Lily scratched herself behind one floppy ear.

"Do bring him back in one piece, countess." Marissa released her grip on Victor and patted him on the chest.

"I shall try," Lady Fenvale said, deadpan.

"Good," Marissa said. "I can forgive you for this … awkwardness, but if something were to happen to Victor, I'd be far less charitable."

"Noted." Lady Fenvale nodded. "Now, if you'll excuse us, we've a schedule to keep."

They exchanged goodbyes, and Marissa disappeared back inside. Lady Fenvale tromped down the narrow stairwell and out into the crowded streets of Kingsforge, with Victor and Lily following on either side. The rest of the city had woken up well before Victor and Marissa did, and so the streets were packed with the barely controlled chaos of bustling city. So many people crammed into the streets brought an inevitable smell: of stale sweat and open sewers, but also of hickory smoke and fresh-baked bread. The business of the city went on all around them; porters hauled their loads, merchants hawked their wares, servants went about their errands, laughing children chased each other, and a clump of old men with nothing better to do provided running commentary on it all. The workings of the city reminded Victor of a machine, albeit a ramshackle, inefficient one.

Lady Fenvale navigated through the fracas without much trouble, though she did have to whistle sharply at Lily whenever the dog started getting too close to a food vendor's stall. Lily splayed her ears back and looked up at Lady Fenvale with a mournful look in her eyes—at which point the countess just sighed and gave in. She bought a paper-wrapped bundle of sausage buns, then tossed one into Lily's drooling jaws.

"Hungry?" she asked, offering Victor one of the fresh-baked buns.

The enticing smell of fresh bread and spiced sausage made Victor's stomach growl in a sound one might have expected from Lily. Lady Fenvale handed him one of the pastries, and Victor scarfed it down only slightly slower than the big dog did. "Thank you," he remembered to add once he'd swallowed the first bite.

"Think nothing of it." Lady Fenvale took a comparatively dainty bite of her own roll. "Last thing I need is a rumor that I can't feed my own staff."

"Something tells me that's going to be the least of our worries." Victor brushed crumbs from his doublet. "Do you think we've got time to swing by the arsenal? I might have some cleaner clothing packed away in the baggage."

"No," Lady Fenvale said flatly. "Perhaps if I'd been able to find you earlier, but we simply don't have the time."

"It's my fault." The words flowed uncontrollably from Victor's mouth, like stampeding cattle escaping their pen. "It's just that, ah, with the wine, and the ... company, one thing led to another, as they tend to do. Or, well, as I'm told things tend to do. This whole affair—oh, that's not the right word—was entirely unexpected on my part. Marissa, er, Master Smith Chalment and I were friends at university, you see. Well, she wasn't a master smith yet at that point. But she was a few years ahead of me in her studies, and she was brilliant even then, which meant she hadn't much reason to take notice of anyone like me. She, er, still doesn't have much reason to, to be honest, so I can only theorize—"

"Victor." Lady Fenvale held up a hand.

"Yes?"

"Have another sausage bun."

Victor gratefully accepted a second snack and set about occupying his mouth with something other than talking.

"Your personal life is of no business of mine, Victor. So long as it doesn't interfere with your duties, you're free to—" She paused, searching for the right (or at least the least suggestive) word. "—associate with whomever you please."

Victor gulped down a mouthful of garlicky sausage and nodded. "I won't. Let it interfere with my duties, that is. Insomuch as it already has, but this entire course of events has caught me entirely by surprise. I promise it won't happen again. Or, uh, at least the part where you've got to set your dog out to track me down, that is."

"Victor?" Lady Fenvale said.

"Yes?"

"Finish your bun."

He looked down at the half-eaten clump of sausage-stuffed bread in his hands. "Right."

"Now, if you're done stammering like a schoolboy, we'd better get moving." Lady Fenvale tossed the last of the sausage buns into Lily's drooling maw and rounded a corner that led to one of the wide, flat avenues built for Cataphracts. From there, they could see all the way to the Steel Circle and the Royal Palace looming behind it like a gilded mountain. "It's time to see what the king wants with us."

By flashing her summons letter (and its unmistakable royal seal), Lady Fenvale was able to make her way past the first few royal guards without much trouble, until a man with a repeating pattern of crossed chamberlain's keys stitched into his tunic led them into the palace proper.

Built on a scale to dwarf Cataphracts, the foyer of the Royal Palace overwhelmed the individual with a glaring reminder of their own insignificance. At least, that was what went through Victor's mind as he stared up at the vaulted ceiling of the central hall, several stories above. Intricately detailed murals stretched across the domed ceiling, painted with heroic pictures of the first Cataphracts of the kingdom bravely slaying enormous, fanged Behemoths. More than a little artistic license had been taken, Victor mused. Most of the machines depicted had their visors open, so as to reveal the heroically muscled and toga-clad men and women helming them. Going into battle with one's visor open, wearing little more than a fancy bedsheet, was certainly an impractical way to go about fighting a battle, but it looked impressive when painted.

The scale was off, too, with the Cataphract captains drawn larger than life, and their Cataphracts scaled down a bit so as not to overshadow them. And then there were the Behemoths themselves: roiling masses of scales and spines, yellow fangs and matted fur, matching no known animal taxonomy. Admittedly, there was something to be said for artistic license, especially considering the last of the Behemoths had been killed centuries before this wing of the Royal Palace had been built.

The mural was at least accurate enough that Victor could identify individual Cataphracts, even from several stories below. At a glance, he picked out *King Leopold's Pardon* leading the *Guilt of Gold* and the *Conflagration* in battle against what appeared to be a cross between an enormous ape and a cuttlefish. After some searching, Victor even saw the *Huntress* depicted in one corner, albeit far cleaner than the actual Cataphract had been in years. In the mural, a dark-haired young man leaned out of the *Huntress'* open visor; Victor wondered if he was some distant ancestor of Lady Fenvale's. A pack of hackleback mastiffs circled around the painted *Huntress'* ankles, silently snarling in the general direction of the nearest Behemoth.

The grandeur of the Royal Palace only increased as one took one's eyes away from the painted ceiling. Every possible surface was decorated: carvings on the support pillars, paintings on the walls, tiled mosaics on the polished floor. Likewise, the palace's guests and staff wore ornate, voluminous finery in a riot of bright colors. Everything about the Royal Palace was larger than life: the architecture, the fashion, the hairstyles. Even the guards; instead of mere men posted at the doors, a pair of gold-plated skirmishers stood guard. Although, to judge from the lack of smoke coming from their exhaust vents, Victor concluded the skirmishers to be just part of the opulent decoration. It would take several minutes to get them moving from a cold start—assuming there was anyone at the controls to begin with.

Various dignitaries and aristocrats milled about the central foyer, arrayed in acres of silk and lace. The crowd skewed older than Marquis Maldrinne's guests; the older courtiers likely hadn't wanted to make the trip all the way out to Maldrinne House. While graying around the temples (or at least beneath the edges of fancy wigs), the assembled nobles were still young enough to strut from one end of the grand foyer to the next, solely for the purpose of seeing others and being seen. Ironically, it was Lady Fenvale's comparatively dull attire that drew the most looks. She tilted her chin up, proud and defiant, and strode across the tiled floor of the foyer, one hand near the hilt of her saber, which was more than enough to ward off any snide remarks—to her face, at least. Victor followed close behind the countess and tried not to think about what rumors were already spreading about Lady Fenvale, murmured behind handkerchiefs and fans.

"This way, Your Excellency." Their guide led them across the grand foyer and through a relatively unobtrusive doorway. As they rounded a corner in the hallway, Victor let out a sigh of relief to finally be out of sight of the courtiers' sneering appraisal.

"His Majesty will receive you shortly. In the meanwhile, would you be so good as to wait in the Map Room," the chamberlain said as he ushered them in. A long table stretched across the room, surrounded by high-backed chairs, with the biggest and most ornate seat at the head of the table reserved for the king himself. Colored tiles along the walls showed a grand map of Leovaix, complete with Cataphract roads in gold inlay and cities represented by silver discs, each one engraved with the sigil of the oldest Cataphract stationed there. At a quick scan, Victor noted the *Huntress'* leaping hound was decidedly absent. Kingsforge's disc, bearing the scroll of *King Leopold's Pardon*, was set in the wall directly behind the Royal Seat. Almost as an afterthought, the edges of the map showed glimpses of the nations bordering Leovaix. Victor counted a handful of Freeholder Principalities (the borders of which had undoubtedly shifted before the map was complete), The Silkmaker Isles (which were shown far smaller than they were said to be), and even a dark gray blotch meant to represent the Theocracy of the Link, tucked away in a corner where anyone sitting in the Royal Seat wouldn't have to look at it.

The chamberlain left them in the Map Room and closed the doors. Victor furrowed his brow, unable to make heads or tails of the royal protocol. It seemed to him that they could have waited just as easily in the Grand Foyer—to summon them to a side room just to leave them there seemed … inefficient. Still, Lady Fenvale wasn't put off by the room shuffling, so Victor could only presume this sort of thing was normal.

He passed time by examining the maps on the walls; the more he looked at them, the more inaccuracies and inconsistencies he spotted. Victor flexed his fingers, wishing he had ink and paper so he could start sketching out something more accurate, or at least write some quick notes correcting the map's errors. He had almost worked up the courage to stick his head out into the hallway to ask a page or footman to bring him some drawing supplies when the doors on the other side of the Map Room opened. Victor and Lady Fenvale turned at the same time, ready to bow to the king—only to freeze in place once they saw who'd come to visit them instead.

"Good to see you, Cousin," said Marquis Maldrinne.

CHAPTER 7

"What the hell do you want?" Lady Fenvale's fingers flexed around the hilt of her saber, but she didn't draw it. Yet. Lily took up a position at the countess' side, while Victor made it a point to stand behind the both of them.

"To help you, of course." Marquis Maldrinne stepped into the room, with Rochen Dunsall close behind. Two men clad in royal scarlet livery followed them in and took up positions at either side of the main door. Guards.

"Try again," Lady Fenvale said.

"Fine." The marquis rolled his eyes. "I want the *Guilt of Gold*'s furnace back. And as I see it, the best way to get it is to help you."

"You have a funny way of helping." Lady Fenvale's eyes flicked to Rochen Dunsall.

"Yes, yes, I stole your thunder—or, rather, Baron Dunsall did." As Marquis Maldrinne revealed Dunsall's new title, the man puffed out his broad chest, showing off his tunic with the *Stalwart*'s tower sigil stitched over the left breast. "But honestly, you should thank me. I've spared you no small amount of dull ceremony—unless you'd prefer to spend several days getting bustled from one salon to another, just so Kingsforge's social elite could chatter at you for hours on end? Honestly, you couldn't even make it through the Summer's Steel festival without causing a row. Left to your own devices, you'd be neck-deep in duels and scandal by now."

Lady Fenvale smiled wolfishly. "A duel does sound appealing."

Dunsall only puffed himself up more, but the two royal guards behind him took a step backward. Marquis Maldrinne just shook his head and leaned against the back of one of the chairs around the long table. "Think ahead, Cousin. I know you'd take quite a bit of satisfaction in carving up Baron Dunsall, but now that you've taken the Cataphract Oath, you're a woman with responsibilities. Do you really think His Majesty would be pleased if his newest Cataphract captains started stabbing each other? One or the both of you would likely wind up in the hospital. Or the morgue. Either way, you'd be no good to the Crown or kingdom in the end. His Majesty doesn't need that sort of embarrassment, believe me."

"I was told the king wanted to see me. Or was that another of your tricks?"

"Oh, he does," Marquis Maldrinne said. "He'll see you shortly after we finish talking. Which is why I recommend you listen very carefully, Cousin."

"More threats?" Lady Fenvale sneered. "You're too late. I've taken the oath. The *Huntress* is mine, and there's nothing you can do about it."

"That's not entirely true," Marquis Maldrinne said offhandedly. "I could press the matter, if I so desired. There are quite a few lawyers who would be happy to debate the particulars of this case on my behalf. Then again, I try to avoid going to court if I can help it."

"After all this, do you really think I'm afraid of a lawsuit?" Lady Fenvale frowned.

"You've convinced me you're not afraid of anything, Cousin. But I've known you long enough to know that you hate being frustrated. And I assure you, from personal experience, there's nothing quite as frustrating—or as expensive, for that matter—as a lawsuit. Even one you're likely to win," Marquis Maldrinne said. "Which is why I've devised an alternative course of action that will benefit the both of us. All you have to do is return the *Guilt of Gold*'s alchemical furnace, and I won't contest your claim to the *Huntress*, or any of the Fenvale holdings, for that matter."

"You can't bribe me with what's already rightfully mine."

"I'm not finished," Marquis Maldrinne huffed. "Let me ask you a question, Diana. Now that the *Huntress* is yours, what will you do next?"

"My plans are none of your concern," Lady Fenvale said.

"Which is another way of saying you don't have any." Marquis Maldrinne looked over the map on the wall and traced the gold line of a Cataphract road with his fingertips. "Have you considered what His Majesty will do with you? He won't assign the *Huntress* to one of the existing crown squadrons, not when there isn't a war to fight. The Brethren are staying put, and the Silkmakers are more interested in our gold than our blood. Perhaps His Majesty will loan you out to one of the Freeholder Princes? They're always squabbling over one thing or another. Just think, the very presence of the *Huntress* might make a difference in determining who gets to graze their sheep on which side of the river."

"I'll take the *Huntress* wherever His Majesty requires," Lady Fenvale said pointedly.

"How dutiful." Marquis Maldrinne turned away from the map.

"You presume to speak for the king?"

"Of course not, no. I'm merely in the unique position of being able to offer His Majesty guidance. Nearly every speck of gold in this palace came from mines I own, you know." The marquis traced his fingers over the gilded inlay on the map once again. "Lucky for you, I'm willing to use my modest influence in your favor."

"Why not save that 'influence' for your lackey?" Lady Fenvale aimed her ire at Rochen Dunsall, but the big man just glared back, unfazed.

"I've got more than one favor to call in, Cousin. Besides, Baron Dunsall has already received his assignment. In a week or so, he is to take the *Stalwart* and take up his new position as Warden of the Northpass Garrison."

"Which is only a few days away from Maldrinne House."

"Quite a convenient coincidence, don't you think?" Marquis Maldrinne smiled. "And I would be happy to arrange something similar for you."

"So you can put me wherever you find convenient? I'll pass."

"Mmm. Canny woman. I knew you'd say that. Which is why I've got a different position for the *Huntress* in mind."

"I'm not interested." Lady Fenvale narrowed her eyes.

"Don't be so dismissive, Cousin. This could be a great opportunity for you. For, as it would happen, the kingdom is currently lacking a Beasthunter-Errant."

Lady Fenvale's sharp laugh echoed off the map-adorned walls. "Don't be ridiculous."

"It was once quite a prestigious title." Marquis Maldrinne pulled one of the chairs away from the table and sat down, casual. "One that was even held by our mutual ancestor, even."

"I remember the play," Lady Fenvale muttered darkly. "But what's the point of a Beasthunter-Errant when there aren't any more wandering Behemoths to hunt?"

"The beasts may be dead, but the title still exists," Marquis Maldrinne noted. "The kingdom holds onto old law like a manor house gathers old furniture. It's true, no one has held the title of Beasthunter-Errant for quite some time. It doesn't come with any holdings, or a salary, or any other perks, which is why nobody's bothered with it for so long. But you, Cousin, you're not interested in that sort of thing. Which is why you're perfect for the job. Without any Behemoths to chase after, you'll be left to your own devices. You can take the *Huntress* wherever you like, with royal approval. In fact, you'll be expected to put the 'errant' into the title. Just roaming about the kingdom, righting wrongs, fighting monsters, saving damsels, what have you. Isn't that what you always wanted? You might even be able to visit your friend Lady Rosalind on occasion."

Lady Fenvale's shoulders tensed, but the marquis didn't seem to notice as he carried on.

"And while it's extremely unlikely that you'll get to slay any giant monsters, you and the *Huntress* can still be useful to His Majesty. As Beasthunter-Errant, you'll be one of the first Cataphract captains mustered if there's trouble on the borders, or if the Brethren start gearing up for another invasion, or—well, you get the idea. But until then, all you'll have to do is march around, fly the banner, and look impressive. Best of all, though, you'll be able to keep yourself far from all the fops and gossips and other hangers-on here at Kingsforge."

"Or at Maldrinne House," Lady Fenvale noted.

"That is a bonus, yes." Marquis Maldrinne steepled his fingers. "For the both of us."

"I still don't trust you," Lady Fenvale said.

"So suspicious." The marquis shook his head. "It's a good thing, then, that I trust you, Cousin. You're stubborn and dangerous, but still a creature of honor. Which is why, as a show of my good faith, I've already given His Majesty the suggestion that he appoint you Beasthunter-Errant. Once you're sworn in, you can return the *Guilt of Gold*'s furnace at your convenience. It's not as if it does you any good to cart an extra alchemical furnace all around the kingdom. You know how valuable they are. Who knows how many unscrupulous villains would try to steal it from you if word got out that you had the *Guilt of Gold*'s furnace just rolling around in your luggage?"

"If word got out that I had the *Guilt of Gold*'s furnace, you'd be a laughingstock."

"Which is why I'd rather settle this matter as soon as possible. Now then—do we have a deal?"

Lady Fenvale's eyes flicked to Rochen Dunsall, to the two royal guardsmen, and then back to her cousin. She pulled in a deep breath and then finally spoke.

"I'll only return the furnace once I have the commission. And —" She held up a finger. "Once I have your word that you'll leave me and mine alone. If that playwright of yours so much as writes a limerick about me—"

"—it will be under his own volition. And even then, I'm highly doubtful he's brave enough to try it. Regardless, I accept your terms." The legs of Marquis Maldrinne's chair squeaked as he pushed it backwards and stood. He fished a pocket watch out of his doublet and flicked the case open. "In any case, we've wasted enough time. You're scheduled to see His Majesty soon, and it would be …

64

inconvenient for the both of us if we were to keep him waiting. Shall we?"

Lady Fenvale didn't move. "You first."

The Hall of the Forge-Throne was one of the oldest in the palace, and as such it hadn't ballooned in scale like later additions such as the Grand Foyer. However, given the hall's age, that just meant that generations of kings had the opportunity to add their own decorations to it, which left every inch of the marble walls packed with dense engravings and sculpture. The Forge-Throne, a thoroughly pillowed chair that looked more comfortable than anything with "forge" in its name should have been, sat on a raised dais at the far end of the room. A circular window directly above the throne let in sunlight, giving the throne (and the royal personage sitting in it) a vaguely divine air.

As the legend went, the Forge-Throne sat above a secret hatch. That hatch led to a tunnel, and that tunnel led to a sprawling network of underground caverns and tunnels. And at the center of those tunnels sat the Kingsforge itself, the miraculous vein of liquid crystal from which the most important city in the world took its name. Leon the Brilliant, first of the Cataphract Kings, had discovered the secret of creating alchemical furnaces and used them to power the first Cataphracts. His descendants guarded the secret for hundreds of years since, leveraging their monopoly on the production of alchemical furnaces to cement their power. It had worked, too, as Leon the Brilliant's descendants had ruled Kingsforge—and therefore, the rest of the world—for centuries. Only the Brethren of the Chain had ever managed to unseat a Cataphract King, and even then their victory was short-lived. Generations ago, the Brethren had held the city for only two years before the rebellion was crushed, the few survivors fleeing to the far reaches of the continent, past even the farthest of the Freeholder Principalities.

Victor didn't know if the Forge-Throne really concealed the door that led all the way to the Kingsforge, but it was certainly guarded like it was. A half-dozen skirmishers, decked out in royal gold and crimson, stood around the edges of the throne room—two of them even had their furnaces lit, thin trails of blue smoke visible against the white marble walls behind them. It must've been a pain to clean, Victor mused. In addition to the small Cataphracts, the Hall of the Forge-Throne was guarded by a platoon of red-clad royal guards, along with twice as many courtiers and other servants. Despite the number of people in the room, it was unusually quiet, allowing each squeak of a boot sole against the polished floor to echo through the room. The quiet broke when the man in the key-pattern doublet announced their arrival:

"Presenting Countess Fenvale, captain of the *Huntress*, and her ... " He paused for just a moment, eyeing Victor and Lily. "Entourage."

"Approach." King Willem the Twelfth waved for them to approach. His clothing, an opulent array of silk, ruffles, and lace trim, gave him the vague air of a fancy pastry—a comparison likely not helped by his round cheeks and afterthought of a chin. His complexion was pale (how much of that was from the powdered makeup, Victor couldn't tell), contrasting the blue of his eyes peeking out amongst the white, like glimpses of clear sky on a cloudy summer day.

Lady Fenvale walked to the center of the room, then swept her broad-brimmed hat off as she bowed. Victor mirrored the gesture, albeit with far less grace and poise. Lily, meanwhile, just sat down on her haunches and glanced around curiously.

"You would bring a dog to my court?" King Willem had a surprisingly deep voice for someone dressed like a wedding cake. Victor didn't know if he should have been relieved he'd escaped the king's notice, or annoyed that, once again, Lily had been acknowledged before he did.

"She does not like to leave me alone, Your Majesty. I find the loyalty comforting." Lady Fenvale kept her head bowed as she spoke.

"I can see the appeal," King Willem said. "Thankfully, I need not rely on a humble animal for such reassurance. I am fortunate, in that I know every one of my subjects possesses the same devotion to me as your hound does to you. Now then—you may rise."

Lady Fenvale stood up straight, and Victor followed suit. He kept his face respectfully neutral, trying not to gawp at the king like some overawed peasant. Now that he was closer to the throne than he'd ever expected to be, Victor realized how flattering the king's official portraits were. It reminded him of the Map Room, with its calculated exaggerations and omissions. It wasn't that King Willem the Twelfth was an ugly man, so much as an unremarkable one. It was hard to fathom that the portly, coiffured man sitting on the Forge-Throne was the direct descendant of the men who built the first Cataphracts and so brought an end to the Behemoth Age.

Victor kept his thoughts to himself.

The king, meanwhile, kept talking. "I had never expected to preside over a Cataphract Oath during my reign. Much less two of them. Should I expect more idealistic young captains to follow you?"

"I am unaware of anyone else ready to take the oath, Your Majesty," Lady Fenvale said.

"As am I." Cushions shifted beneath King Willem as he leaned back on his throne and crossed his legs, impatiently bobbing one booted foot. "But, back to the matter at hand. You are due a commission, and I have thought of the perfect one for you. Since you captain the *Huntress*, it is only fitting that your title reflect your Cataphract's name. Therefore, I appoint you, Countess Fenvale, as Beasthunter-Errant."

The king rubbed his hands together, pleased with his idea. A snapping of royal fingers summoned a pair of young men in green scribes' robes, carrying a portable desk between them. As they set the desk down beside the throne, Victor caught a glimpse of the document laid out upon it, already covered in ornate calligraphy and wax seals. The king held his hand out for a pen, reverently provided by one of his scribes, at which point King Willem the Twelfth applied his official signature to the parchment with no small amount of flourish.

"Countess Diana Fenvale, you are hereby charged with the protection of the Throne, the Kingdom, and all loyal subjects within from any and all threats, be they man or beast. To this end, you are now granted the discretion to take your machine, the duelist-class Cataphract *Huntress*, anywhere such threats to the peace might be."

The king exchanged the pen for the parchment, now finalized with his signature.

"Approach the throne and accept your commission, Countess Fenvale."

Lady Fenvale stepped forward, and the king stood up to lay the parchment into her outstretched hands. She bowed, deeply. "Thank you, Your Majesty."

"You are most welcome, Countess. Now, go forth and ... err." King Willem turned away from Lady Fenvale and clapped his hands as he looked to a cluster of assembled advisors—a clump of well-dressed men and women that included Marquis Maldrinne. "What's next on the schedule?"

Lady Fenvale bowed again and then backed away from the Forge-Throne. Just as she made it back to Victor and Lily, a man with a leather valise under his arm entered the hall. One of the chamberlains cleared his throat and announced him.

"Duke Astello, of the North Coast."

To Victor's surprise, the man was even more unkempt than he was, with mud and road dust still spattered across his boots and clothing. He breathed heavily, as if he'd sprinted through the palace, if not the whole city. A small commotion rippled through the court; Duke Astello's sudden arrival was obviously not part of the day's scheduled business. Victor stayed in place behind Lady Fenvale, remaining quiet, grateful that some new business had come to distract the court from Lady Fenvale's commission.

"It is good to see you, Nephew," King Willem said. "But you should have sent word ahead, so I could prepare a suitable reception—and you could have made yourself more presentable."

"My apologies for my slovenly state, Your Majesty." Lord Astello bowed low, and Victor could swear he saw a bead of sweat drop from the lord's forehead and fall to the polished floor. "The news was urgent, and my father bid me to speak with you directly."

"Well then, speak. What's so important that you had to ride all the way to Kingsforge with such reckless haste?"

Duke Astello stood up, showing how pale his face was—and not from makeup.

"Your Majesty, we've sighted a Behemoth."

CHAPTER 8

Despite the pomp and frippery, King Willem the Twelfth had at least some leadership skills.

Namely delegation.

"Let the Beasthunter-Errant step forward." With a single wave of his hand, the king silenced the murmurings that rippled through the throne room. With another gesture, he bid Lady Fenvale to approach the throne. The newly commissioned Beasthunter-Errant stood up straighter as she found herself the center of the court's attention for the second time.

The king leaned forward and looked the countess up at down, appraising her worthiness. "Consider yourself lucky, Countess. Here's an opportunity to show your merit if there ever was one. When can you have your duelist ready?"

"The *Huntress* can leave at first light tomorrow, Your Majesty. Or even earlier, if need be."

With all eyes on Lady Fenvale and the king, no one saw Victor wince. Admittedly, having the *Huntress* ready to go so soon was possible, but he certainly wouldn't have the time to give her the sort of complete overhaul that he had hoped to. Every minute spent in the Royal Palace ate into Victor's schedule—but he knew he couldn't leave the court until he was formally dismissed.

"Mmm." King Willem steepled his long, ring-laden fingers and turned his attention to the dust-spattered Duke Astello. "Nephew —this Behemoth. Has it made landfall?"

"Not to my knowledge, Your Majesty. According to the reports we received, the beast was last spotted a day's sail from the mainland."

"And you're sure it wasn't just some sort of whale?" asked the king.

"Whales don't sink tradeships, Your Majesty. A fisherman saw the Behemoth ram a merchant galley from below and drag it beneath the waves. The ship's figurehead washed ashore the next day, along with a few crates of cargo. My father sent his personal guard out on a ship to search for survivors, but they have not been back since."

"Has my brother made any other preparations? Besides sending you here, that is."

"He's called up the *Challenge*, and the *Major Simon*— and, of course, he has the *Tender Mercy of Queen Jeriel* at his disposal." Each Cataphract Duke Astello listed was a formidable one, with an honorable record, but the coast was simply too long to be guarded by a mere three Cataphracts."They've likely rallied at my father's castle by now."

"Then the *Huntress* shall join them," King Willem decreed, looking past his nephew to focus on Lady Fenvale again. "You shall depart for the North Coast at first light tomorrow. Once you are there, Countess, you shall take command of the hunt and do everything in your power to protect the kingdom. Do you understand your mission?"

Lady Fenvale nodded, face stony and resolute. "I do."

"Excellent." King Willem nodded. "Then go, make whatever preparations you need. In the meanwhile, Duke Astello and I shall discuss the details of this Behemoth sighting. Privately. Good hunting, Countess. You and the rest of the court are dismissed."

With that, King Willem stood and walked out of the Hall of the Forge-Throne. With a wave of a lace-shrouded hand, he signaled Duke Astello (and half a dozen other senior courtiers besides) to follow. Notably, Marquis Maldrinne wasn't among them. Victor supposed the term "private" meant something different when one wore the crown. Everyone else merely bowed and stepped out of the king's way. Once the monarch left, the rest of the court descended into a low din of gossipy chaos. Before anyone thought to ask him questions, Victor took refuge in Lady Fenvale's proverbial shadow.

"Ah—Countess Fenvale?" Victor spoke quickly, as he always did when he was nervous. Which seemed to be all the time, lately. "Not that I would presume to tell you what to do, but if we're going to leave tomorrow we'll need to get back to the Arsenal as soon as—"

"We will." Lady Fenvale set off across the hall with purpose in her stride. "But there's something I need to take care of, first."

It didn't take her long to find Marquis Maldrinne and Rochen Dunsall. The two men were talking with a handful of officers and dignitaries, who discreetly extracted themselves from the marquis' company once they saw Lady Fenvale storming over with a no-quarter scowl on her face.

"Ah. Cousin." Marquis Maldrinne smiled politely. "Let's find someplace quieter to chat. Follow me."

He turned and walked out of the room without waiting for an answer. Rochen Dunsall proved not as brave as his patron, as he uneasily looked over his shoulder every few steps, unwilling to turn his back on Lady Fenvale and Lily for long.

"Stop fretting." Lady Fenvale kept her voice low and level. "If I draw steel on you, Baron Dunsall, I'll make sure you see it coming."

Dunsall muttered a few un-baronlike obscenities beneath his breath and kept walking. Marquis Maldrinne led the bunch of them to the map room—though this time without the two royal guards as an escort. They still made an odd group: three aristocrats, a rumpled alchemical engineer, and a very large dog.

As soon as the door to the Map Room closed, Lady Fenvale bore down on her cousin. "How did you know?" She jabbed an accusatory finger into Marquis Maldrinne's chest—which Victor supposed was better than a dagger, at least.

"I'm just as shocked as you are." Marquis Maldrinne planted his feet and gently pushed Lady Fenvale's finger away. Dunsall, meanwhile, glared at Victor and Lily but remained silent.

"I don't believe you." Lady Fenvale stepped back.

"Think about it." Marquis Maldrinne gestured at the map on the wall. "Duke Astello rode here straight from the North Coast, and killed at least two horses while he did it. There's no possible way I could have gotten the news ahead of time. And even if I did, don't you think I'd use that knowledge to my advantage? If I'd had the foreknowledge, I could have had Dunsall installed as Beasthunter-Errant, not you. Then he would be the center of attention."

"Unless this whole charade is just an overcomplicated plot to humiliate me," Lady Fenvale said.

"You flatter me, Cousin. But even I'm not influential enough to get the likes of Duke Astello to ride hell-for-leather across half the kingdom, much less summon a Behemoth from the sea. Assuming there's one at all, and it's not a hoax." The marquis ran his finger over the map on the wall, from the North Coast down to Kingsforge. "That the duke is here at all is telling—he'd never raise such a ruckus over the ranting of some drunk fisherman. Whatever's happening, Duke Astello thinks it's so important that he had to come personally instead of sending a messenger. Still—this can be beneficial to the both of us, Diana. You, obviously, get to march off with your Cataphract in defense of the kingdom. And, since I'm the one who gave His Majesty the idea of making you Beasthunter-Errant, your successes will reflect well on me."

"When you put it that way, I've half a mind to make a hash of it on purpose."

"Please." Marquis Maldrinne rolled his eyes. "We both know you won't. You've spent your whole life playing at heroics, and this is your chance to do it officially. You'd never throw that away just to spite me. You're too honorable."

"I will do my duty," she finally said.

"I expected no less." Marquis Maldrinne clasped his hands behind his back and rocked back on his heels. "Now then, there's still the matter of the *Guilt of Gold*'s furnace—"

"You really think I'll return it now?"

"Indeed I do. I came through on my end of the deal, after all. Not to mention that, if there's one Behemoth lurking about, there's a more-than-likely chance there will be others. And if that's the case, isn't it in the kingdom's best interests to have every possible

Cataphract ready to fight? And isn't it your duty as Beasthunter-Errant to take every precaution necessary for the protection of the kingdom?"

"This could still be a hoax," Lady Fenvale said.

"It could be. Which is why you need to be careful." Marquis Maldrinne shrugged. "In fact, a so-called Behemoth sighting would be the perfect excuse for Prince Edval to rally his troops before doing something … brash. It's nearly tradition for royal siblings to plot against each other."

"You would think of that," Lady Fenvale muttered.

"Indeed, I would. Thankfully, so did His Majesty. Did you notice how he put you in charge of the hunt? He's not sending you to assist. He's sending you to lead, despite the fact you haven't been Beasthunter-Errant for more than an hour yet. You're an unknown factor, Cousin—a disruptive one. Your presence alone will be enough to throw off whatever schemes Prince Edval has going."

"If there is a scheme."

"There may or may not be a Behemoth, but there's always a scheme, Cousin. Which is yet another reason you must return what's rightfully mine. If there is a war brewing, the *Guilt of Gold* will be there to protect the Crown, same as you."

"What admirable loyalty," Lady Fenvale said, deadpan.

"If you doubt my loyalty, then think about my self-interest. You don't even know how much money I've invested in the throne. If King Willem's deposed by his brother, or eaten by a Behemoth, or otherwise removed from power, things will get … inconvenient. Which is why I am going to do everything I possibly can in order to keep the peace. So while our motives may be different, Diana, our goals are the same. Now, will you give me the furnace, or are you going to waste time by making things even more difficult than necessary?"

"Fine," Lady Fenvale muttered, and consoled herself by reaching down with her left hand to pet Lily's side. Even still, she kept her right hand, her sword hand, free. "Meet me at the Royal Arsenal at midnight, and I'll have the furnace ready. Until then, stay out of my way. I've got work to do."

News of Duke Astello's Behemoth traveled fast; by the time Lady Fenvale and Victor made it to the Royal Arsenal, it was already in an uproar.

"I'm going to speak with General Barrowgale and see what he thinks of all this. Make the *Huntress* ready while I'm gone," Lady Fenvale ordered, then hopped out of the carriage before it even stopped moving. Lily followed after her, and the two strode off for the captains' wing. Afraid of breaking his neck on the cobblestones, Victor waited an extra minute for the carriage to come to a complete halt before he climbed out. This gave enough time for a handful of nearby apprentices to notice his arrival and immediately start barraging him with questions.

"Is it really a Behemoth?"

"What did the king say?"

"Who was the last Beasthunter-Errant?"

"How can we help?"

At least Victor could answer that question. To his mild amazement, he found the other engineers of the Royal Arsenal actually listening to him and doing as he told them.

Even with the eager help of the Royal Arsenal crew at his disposal, Victor soon realized the key difference between what he wanted to do and what he could do. There wasn't enough time to strip the *Huntress* down to her frame for a full overhaul, but with the added help, he could at least ensure that her joints were oiled, her exhaust vents cleared, her control cables tightened, and her sword sharpened.

Victor clambered up and down the scaffolding like an indecisive monkey, trying to supervise each task simultaneously. As much as he wanted to focus on the *Huntress*, Victor periodically had to descend from the scaffold to haggle with the Royal Arsenal's quartermasters. Argument by argument, he secured the supplies the *Huntress* would need for a Behemoth hunt: spools of extra cable, lengths of brass piping, spare bolts of every size, kegs of thick gear oil, and a long list of other equipment besides.

Victor had the most trouble in securing a wagon large enough to carry everything he wanted to bring. He eventually compromised with a smaller wagon, carrying less equipment. He thought about assembling multiple supply wagons for a whole caravan, but decided against it; the more gear they brought, the slower they'd travel, and time was of the essence with a Behemoth potentially lurking off the coast.

While the other journeymen and engineers hadn't worked on the *Huntress* specifically, her design was similar enough to other duelist-class Cataphracts that they were able to perform the basic maintenance without much trouble. On the positive side, the superficial repairs at least meant that nobody would get a deeper look at the decidedly nonstandard modifications Victor had made, or at the box hidden beneath the *Huntress'* helm-seat.

Hours passed, and Victor's back and shoulders soon ached from his constant climbing up and down the *Huntress'* scaffolding. Amidst the bustle and confusion, Victor ducked into the *Huntress'* open visor under pretext of inspecting the duelist's control levers. To his great relief, the *Guilt of Gold*'s alchemical furnace was still in its box, secured beneath the *Huntress'* helm-seat. Victor stuffed the box into a canvas bag, slung it across his shoulder, and slipped away from the *Huntress'* helm without anyone so much as giving him a second look. It'd be odd for a Cataphract's chief engineer not to double- and triple-check the instruments and levers at the helm, after all. The extra weight of the alchemical furnace didn't weigh him down too much, and the other engineers were kept busy enough not to ask questions about what was in the bag.

One by one, the engineers and journeymen finished their tasks, and Victor made it a point to double-check their work once they did. Once he confirmed everything was to his standards, he released the other engineers to their own tasks; the *Huntress* wasn't the only

Cataphract being readied. Soon, Victor realized that he was the only one standing on the *Huntress'* scaffolding.

Stiff-legged, Victor went down the ladder one last time and walked out in front of the *Huntress* so he could survey the work. At a glance, the *Huntress* looked the same as she had before: powerful and imposing, albeit with the unpainted pieces of her armor contrasting the enameled white of the older pieces. But that didn't matter; the real test would be in the smoothness of her stride, the burn of her furnace, the steadiness of her sword. But that would have to wait until they set out the next morning.

"She needs paint." Marissa set a keg-sized bucket down on the cobblestones beside Victor.

"What?" Victor said, turning to look at her. The master smith had pulled on an old, oversized smock and balanced a pair of paintbrushes tied to long poles on her shoulder, like a pikeman on the march.

"The *Huntress*. She'll need a fresh coat of paint before you march tomorrow." Marissa planted the butt end of her pole-brush on the ground. "You should know by now that appearance is everything, especially here in the capital. Everyone's going to expect something out of the old legends, with a glorious, immaculate war machine stomping out to fight the evil Behemoths, so the *Huntress* will need to look the part."

"I hadn't considered that."

"I knew you wouldn't," Marissa said.

"Thank you. But—" Victor crouched down so he could take the lid off the bucket and peer at its contents. The paint inside was a pristine white, but it also looked thin and watery. "I don't think this has the right consistency."

"Oh, it doesn't," Marissa said. "But it'll go on fast and last just long enough for your countess to look suitably impressive when she departs. Provided it doesn't rain, that is."

"Sounds like another metaphor for high society," Victor said as he stood.

"You're catching on quick!" Marissa winked and handed him a paintbrush. "I knew you were smart."

True to Marissa's word, the paint went on quick and easy enough, even though it tended to run and pool into the various recesses of the *Huntress'* armor. Victor tried not to think about cleaning paint spatters out of her joints later. As they slathered whitewash over the *Huntress'* armor plating, Marissa passed the time with idle conversation, taking Victor's mind off the work, and off the anxiety that came from gearing up for the *Huntress'* first campaign in years.

"Remember the time Professor Dorrett started feuding with the mathematician-general over—what was it?"

"The philosophical nature of zero," Victor said, remembering the angry exchange of pamphlets and broadsheets, in which the two academics tore into each other as logically and politely as such an argument required.

"That's it! Literally a fuss over nothing." Marissa laughed as she dragged her paintbrush over the edge of the *Huntress'* breastplate. "Did you know he almost challenged the mathematician-general to a duel?"

"Really?" Victor angled his own pole-brush downward to dip it into the bucket of whitewash. "I never heard about it."

"I imagine he didn't mention it to the apprentices, not after I talked him out of it at the last minute. I heard the mathematician-general's secretary did the same, and so they managed to settle the matter without coming to an official duel." Marissa's paintbrush never stopped moving as she spoke. "It's a good thing we did, too—can you imagine those two old men flailing at each other with swords?"

Victor shook his head and laughed. "I'd prefer not to."

"Oh, you're no fun." Marissa shifted her grip on her pole-brush.

"I've seen enough swordplay in the last few months to last me a lifetime, to be honest," Victor said.

"You'd better get used to it." Marissa's voice dropped to a more serious register. "Especially running around with Countess Fenvale."

"Yes, well. I'd hoped we'd—er, which is to say, Countess Fenvale and I—wouldn't have to worry about that sort of thing anymore, now that she's got an official commission. All she's got to do is slay monsters, and all I've got to do is make sure the *Huntress* is ready for it."

"That's optimistic, even for you." Marissa stepped back, taking her paintbrush away from the Cataphract. "There we are, a nice coat of white paint. Much better, don't you think, Victor?"

Victor lowered his own brush to get a better look at their handiwork. Sure enough, the fresh coat of paint had transformed the *Huntress* from a battle-scarred veteran to a white-gleaming champion. At least, that's the way it looked from a distance; the closer Victor got, the more he could see where the paint was uneven and where the tint of the whitewash didn't quite match the pearly enamel of the *Huntress'* older armor plating. But the hour was late, his back was aching, and the paint wasn't nearly as vital as all the other maintenance performed over the last few hours.

"It'll do," Victor said, and let the pole-brush clatter to the ground.

"You look exhausted." Marissa wrapped an arm around Victor's waist to pull him close, despite the grease and paint spattering his clothes. Then again, her own painting smock was only marginally cleaner. Victor shifted the bag holding the *Guilt of Gold*'s alchemical furnace to the side so it wouldn't jab Marissa in the ribs as she leaned in close. Very, very close.

Marissa's breath washed over Victor's ear. "Why don't we find someplace comfortable and—"

"Victor has other plans for the evening," Lady Fenvale said flatly.

Were it not for Marissa's arm around his waist, Victor would've jumped. But, with Marissa steadying him, he was able to turn and bow politely, as if Lady Fenvale making an unannounced appearance was an everyday occurrence. Which, he realized, it was. At least all parties involved were dressed this time around. Lady Fenvale still wore her black, broad-brimmed hat and maroon captain's tunic, now with a short cape added to the ensemble. She kept the cape clear of her left side, so as not to cover the *Huntress'* leaping-hound sigil stitched into her tunic—or the saber hanging from her hip, for that matter. Lily, of course, stood next to the countess, loyal and slobbery and intimidating as ever.

"Of course he does." Marissa squeezed Victor again, then planted a quick kiss on his cheek. "In that case, I'll let him go. But do be careful. The both of you. It'd be a pity if Kingsforge's newest heroes got themselves killed while out skulduggering."

Victor blinked. "We're not—er—it's—I mean, uh. What makes you think it's skulduggery?"

Marissa rolled her eyes, then set about collecting the paintbrushes, poles, and leftover whitewash. "There are only two reasons why anyone would be prowling around at this hour, and it's obvious you don't fit the countess' … preferences."

Lady Fenvale arched a brow.

Victor wrung his paint-stained hands. "I, er—honestly I wouldn't say that I'm anyone's type." He paused. "Except, er, yours, Marissa? Obviously. For, uh, some reason that I'm not entirely sure of yet."

"I'd explain, but it might take a while." Marissa winked at Victor.

"And we don't have the time," Lady Fenvale said.

"That too." Marissa shouldered the painting gear. "I'll get out of your way. I'm sure this is one of those things I'm better off not knowing about."

"It is," Lady Fenvale said.

"In that case, I bid the both of you good night. Happy hunting." Marissa dipped down into a paint-spattered curtsy and walked off with the painting equipment. She left a trail of small white drops as she departed, but Victor figured a good rain would wash them away before long.

Lady Fenvale kept quiet until the master smith disappeared from sight, then released a long breath. "You have—" She reined herself in, then glanced around in case someone was lurking, eavesdropping. "—what my cousin wants?"

"I do, yes." Victor nodded and shifted the bag holding the *Guilt of Gold*'s alchemical furnace, reassured by the weight tugging it down.

"Good." The countess reached beneath her cape and produced a long-barreled pistol. She flipped the flintlock around to grip it by the barrel and offered it to Victor. "Take this."

Victor stared at the weapon and bit the inside of his cheek. "Is that really necessary?"

"I hope it won't be," Lady Fenvale said. "But with everything that's going on, we're better safe than sorry. Honestly, I should have given you a gun ages ago. You do know how to use one, don't you?"

Tentatively, Victor accepted the weapon, keeping his finger well away from the trigger and the muzzle pointed at the ground. To his relief, he noted the hammer was uncocked, left in a safe—or at least safer position. "I, er—I'm familiar with the mechanical principles. Hammer. Trigger. Spark. Bang."

"That will have to do," Lady Fenvale said. "Stick the pistol in your belt for now—only fire if you absolutely have to. Understand?"

Victor nodded understanding and carefully tucked the weapon into his belt, managing to do so without shooting himself or dropping his pants. The gun felt even heavier than the *Guilt of Gold*'s alchemical furnace tugging the shoulder strap of his bag.

Once Victor had the pistol tucked under his belt, Lady Fenvale started off across the Royal Arsenal and beckoned for him to follow. "If things go sour, run for the *Huntress*. Lily and I should be able to handle most anything my cousin might try, but—"

"What do you think the marquis has planned?"

"I don't know." Lady Fenvale hitched her swordbelt a notch tighter. "But damned if I won't be ready for it."

CHAPTER 9

The waxing moon cast an eerie silver sheen over the Royal Arsenal. With the cauldron-lamps extinguished and the shouting crews gone for the day, it was unnervingly quiet, save for the clack of bootheels upon the cobblestones.

Two men, one taller and broader than the other, stood in the center of the main plaza. Even in the darkness, there was no mistaking Rochen Dunsall's bulk. Marquis Maldrinne had a far less distinct silhouette, but Victor doubted the marquis had sent anyone else. By the look of it, the two had come alone, though there were innumerable places to hide in the long shadows of the towering Cataphracts and the machinery used to maintain them.

Victor kept looking nervously over his shoulder, while Lady Fenvale kept her eyes forward. Lily's nose twitched, but Lady Fenvale quieted her dog's rumbling growl with a short, quiet whistle.

"You're early." Marquis Maldrinne tilted the brim of his hat up as they approached. Beside him, Dunsall tapped his fingers against the pommel of the sword on his hip, impatient and dangerous.

"Are you complaining?" Lady Fenvale asked. Victor, meanwhile, clasped both hands on the strap of his canvas bag so as to keep his hands away from the pistol in his belt.

"Quite the opposite. The sooner we get this settled, the better. You did bring the furnace, yes?" Marquis Maldrinne asked.

"Not everyone's as devious as you are, Cousin." Lady Fenvale snapped her fingers. "Victor. Hand it over."

"Of course." Victor unslung the canvas bag and stepped forward, offering it at arm's length.

Dunsall grabbed hold of the strap and pulled it from his hand. The big man peered inside, then looked up at Marquis Maldrinne and let out an affirmative-sounding grunt. "It's here."

The marquis' white teeth shone in the moonlight as he smiled. "Thank you, Cousin. Perhaps this can serve as a fresh start between us. I may have wronged you before, but—"

"Spare me," Lady Fenvale growled. "You've got what you want, now call off your lackeys."

Marquis Maldrinne's smile faltered. "My what?"

"The men you've got lurking behind the training armatures." She nodded to a spot some distance behind and to the right of Marquis Maldrinne. Victor strained his eyes to look, and barely saw something move within the shadow of the wood-and-rope machines. "Lily spotted them as soon as we got here."

The big dog growled again and fixed her eyes on a point in the shadows further down the plaza.

Marquis Maldrinne chanced a look over his shoulder, then wrapped his gloved fingers around the hilt of his rapier. "Baron Dunsall and I came alone."

"I told you we can't trust her." Dunsall yanked his own sword from its scabbard and leveled its point at the center of Lady Fenvale's chest. "She's probably called up some of her father's old friends."

"Do you really think I'd need more than my sword and my dog to deal with the two of you?" Lady Fenvale neatly stepped back, and her saber materialized in her hand. She kept the blade angled defensively, not moving to strike at Dunsall. Yet. Lily splayed her ears back and bared her teeth in a snarl, while Victor made it a point to stay behind the both of them. With a gut-churning epiphany, Victor thought to look over his shoulder—and sure enough, he saw several figures in gray hooded cloaks emerge from hiding spots behind them.

"Uh," Victor said.

"Not to mention the fact that my cousin doesn't have that many friends." Marquis Maldrinne couldn't help himself from flinging the verbal barb.

"While you have no shortage of enemies," Lady Fenvale said.

"Er." Victor fumbled his pistol out of his belt. "If I may have a word—"

"You may not, you useless idiot," Dunsall snapped. "Shut up while your betters are talking."

"Come off it, baron." Lady Fenvale made the title an epithet. She turned her head just enough to look at Victor from the corner of her eye. "What is it?"

"We're surrounded," Victor blurted. He turned fully around and faced the cloak-wearing men closing in on them. With both hands around the grip of the flintlock, Victor kept the muzzle from shaking too badly. The hooded figures stopped advancing and fanned out into a circle, surrounding the group. Lady Fenvale wheeled around, trying to keep an eye on the hooded men and Marquis Maldrinne at the same time.

"Might I suggest a truce, Cousin?" Marquis Maldrinne faced down the cloaked marauders coming in from the other direction, whipping the point of his rapier up. Dunsall took up a position beside him, blade at the ready. The four of them (five, counting Lily) formed an uneasy ring, weapons pointed outward as easily double their number of cloaked figures came to a halt just outside of sword range. They all stared at each other for a long, terrible moment, while Lily growled deep enough that Victor could feel the vibrations through the soles of his boots. Metal flashed in the moonlight as the hooded men drew long, thin knives. Finally, one of them spoke.

"No witnesses."

Then, chaos.

Victor pulled hard on the trigger, only to realize he hadn't cocked his flintlock. Before he could pull the hammer back to firing position, the cloaked man he'd been aiming at flicked a hand forward. A length of steel chain streamed from beneath his cloak, and the weighted end tangled around Victor's wrists, binding them together. The man on the other end yanked hard, and Victor staggered off-balance, falling to his face. He rolled over just in time to see his captor closing in, keeping the chain taut with one hand while raising a wickedly pointed dagger in the other.

Victor choked out a terrified, undignified cry—but the knife never fell. Instead, Lady Fenvale lunged forward, slashing with her saber. Her first cut knocked the knife out of the cloaked man's hand, her second hit him across the chest. The man staggered back a step, then collapsed. Blood spouted into the air, dark as oil in the moonlight.

Victor couldn't tell if the man was dead or merely wounded, but the chain around his wrists went slack all the same. Lady Fenvale kept moving, falling in among the cloaked men, hacking away at them with her saber. Lily followed close at her heels and snapped at anyone who tried to attack her mistress from behind. The unknown assassins lashed out with long knives and longer chains, but Lady Fenvale expertly batted the attacks away before they could land. Lily clamped her jaws around the knife arm of one of the attackers, and Victor could hear the sound of bone breaking over the man's high-pitched scream.

Free of the chain, Victor stumbled to his feet and cocked the hammer of his pistol. Thusly armed, he started looking for a target—or better yet, an escape route. But with the swirling melee all around, Victor feared he'd be cut down the moment he set out on his own, like a sheep separated from the rest of its flock, helpless against marauding wolves.

Marquis Maldrinne and Rochen Dunsall fought back-to-back, holding their assailants at bay. A chain tangled around the marquis' rapier, but he pulled a dagger from his boot and flung it into his opponent's face with his free hand in a smooth, practiced motion. The hooded man swore and staggered back, dropping his weapon. More of the hooded men converged on Dunsall— understandable, since he was the biggest man there. Two of the assassins harried the baron with feints and slashes, while a third circled around to his left, angling his knife towards the big man's exposed side.

"Look out!" Victor blurted as soon as he realized what was going on.

"Bastard!" Dunsall swore and kicked his assailant in the chest. The assassin staggered back, coughing—and then whipped his head up, sighting in on Victor. Easier prey.

The cloaked man lunged, slashing with his knife, and the engineer threw his left arm up in a reflexive attempt to defend himself. The razor-edged blade sliced through Victor's sleeve and into the muscle of his forearm, sending a blinding flash of red-hot pain through his body.

Victor's voice cracked as he screamed, though the sound was overwhelmed by the deafening boom of a pistol. The assassin's hood fell back enough to reveal a dazed expression on his face as he looked down at the spreading red stain in the center of his chest. Victor, meanwhile, had an equally bewildered look as he stared at the smoking barrel of the flintlock in his hand and realized he must have pulled the trigger by accident.

"Good shot!" Rochen Dunsall said, as if the two of them were out shooting grouse, not fighting for their lives.

"Thank you?" Victor let the spent pistol tumble out of his shaking fingers.

The remaining assassins fell back, fleeing from Lady Fenvale's ferocity and the attention a pistol shot would no doubt bring. Lily took off after one of them, snapping her jaws shut around his trailing cloak. Cloth tore—and then a "pop" echoed out over the Royal Arsenal as the assassin threw a fist-sized bundle of cloth to the ground. A cloud of stinging, red-tinted smoke burst outward to cover his retreat. Lily whined and backed away, shaking her head and sneezing violently. The assassin bolted into the shadows as the puff of foul-smelling smoke dissipated.

"Lily!" Lady Fenvale ran to her dog's side, then grabbed the hackleback mastiff's collar to pull her away from the acrid smoke. "Damn it, someone get some water—"

"The dog will live, Cousin. Unlike these bastards." Marquis Maldrinne wiped his blade clean on one of the dead men's cloaks. "Now pull yourself together. We've got more important matters to attend to."

Lady Fenvale tightened her grip on her still-bloody saber. "Don't give me orders like I'm—"

"Not orders," Marquis Maldrinne said. "Observations. Starting with the fact that your engineer's bleeding more than that stupid beast of yours."

Lady Fenvale blinked, finally looking over at Victor. "Oh," she said. "Are you—"

Victor clasped his right hand over his wounded left arm and tried a shaky smile to match the others' bravado. "I—I don't think it hit any major arteries, though medicine was never really a focus of my studies."

"Let me see, friend." Rochen Dunsall sheathed his saber and tromped over to loom over Victor. The engineer hesitated, and Dunsall rolled his eyes. "I've been in enough scrapes to know what'll kill you and what won't."

"In another life, Baron Dunsall could have been a surgeon," Marquis Maldrinne noted dryly.

Hesitant, Victor held his wounded arm out for Dunsall's inspection. The bearlike man squinted in the darkness, then pulled a long dagger. Victor heard Lady Fenvale suck in a breath, ready to bark out another threat or warning. Before she could, the baron cut away Victor's bloody sleeve. At least it wasn't much of a loss; Victor's clothing was already smeared with dark grease and white paint anyway. Without the sleeve in the way, Dunsall peered at Victor's wound, and snorted.

"It's a scratch." He put his blade away and produced a clean handkerchief, which he wrapped around Victor's arm. "Won't even need any stitches, most like. Drink some brandy for the pain, keep your bandages clean to keep out the rot, and in a few weeks you might have a scar worth lying about."

"I … I'll take that into consideration." Victor flexed the fingers of his left hand, relieved to find they still moved normally. The wound still throbbed, but not cripplingly so. "Thank you."

"Think nothing of it." Dunsall straightened up from where he hunched over Victor's arm. "You kept one of those bastards from sticking me. Might've saved my life, friend. Least I can do is patch you up in return."

"It wasn't that long ago you tried to shoot me."

"And you nearly crushed me flat with the *Guilt of Gold*. But I'm professional enough not to hold a grudge." Dunsall smiled, then pulled the makeshift bandage around Victor's arm tight enough to make him doubt the veracity of the baron's words.

"Now then." Marquis Maldrinne sheathed his rapier as he spoke to Lady Fenvale. "I'm not naive enough to expect you to like me, Cousin, but even you're smart enough to realize we've got a common enemy."

"Do we?" Lady Fenvale put her own sword away and used the cuff of her shirt to wipe pepper dust from Lily's face. The hackleback mastiff sat down and whined, her ferocity drained away.

"We did kill several of them." Marquis Maldrinne walked over to one of the three gray-clad corpses left on the ground. "But the others got away to tell their friends. If they weren't angry at you before, they are now."

"And who in blazes are they?" Dunsall asked.

"A good question." Marquis Maldrinne turned one of the bodies—the man Victor had shot—over with his boot. He crouched down to get a better look and held up a length of chain with a gloved hand, examining the weapon.

"If that bastard hadn't hit Lily with a smoke bomb, she could track them down—" Lady Fenvale finished wiping Lily's face, and the dog sneezed again.

"So they're professionals." Marquis Maldrinne let the steel chain drop to the ground. "Or at least smart enough to plan ahead." He tugged the edge of the dead man's cloak back, then looked over at Victor. "You. Come here," he ordered.

The casual authority in the marquis' voice made Victor move before the engineer even really registered it. "Er, yes?" Victor said as he walked over, making it a point to look at anything but the gory ruin of the dead man's chest.

"What sort of tools are these?" Marquis Maldrinne pointed to a bundle tied to the assassin's belt.

Cradling his wounded arm, Victor sank down to one knee beside the corpse and tried not to dwell on the mixed smells of blood and gunpowder all around him. Victor found himself wishing he was the one who'd gotten a faceful of pepper smoke instead of Lily as he focused on the bundle of tools. Despite the gloom, he had no trouble in identifying them. "Torsion wrenches, cable snips, a bolt hammer—"

"Didn't think alchemical engineers could fight like that," Dunsall said.

"We can't. Or, uh, I can't. It's not exactly in university curriculum." Victor rubbed at his wounded arm and forced himself to look at the dead man's face, still frozen in a rictus of surprise. "And I don't recognize any of these men from the Royal Arsenal, either. Which isn't to say I've met everyone here, but—"

"Saboteurs, then," Marquis Maldrinne concluded.

Victor's stomach turned and his mouth went dry. "I need to get back to the *Huntress*, make sure she hasn't been damaged."

"We will." Lady Fenvale stepped up beside Victor and squeezed his shoulder. "Unless anyone has anything else to add?"

"It doesn't bloody make sense." Rochen Dunsall kicked another of the dead assassins. "The Royal Arsenal's big enough that they could've sabotaged a dozen Cataphracts without us noticing. Why would they bother with us?"

"Maybe they didn't plan on it?" Victor carefully put the dead man's tools back into their pouches as a gesture of respect. Even still, his mind raced, arranging the facts and forming hypotheses. "These men knew enough about Cataphract engineering to bring the right tools with them to do the most damage with the least effort. It stands to reason that they also knew enough about alchemical engineering to know how much something like the *Guilt of Gold*'s furnace is worth. So it's a crime of ... opportunity, I guess?"

"If they had the tools, why not just steal the furnace from one of the other Cataphracts?" Lady Fenvale's expression darkened. "If they've stolen anything from the *Huntress*—"

Victor shook his head. "The alchemical furnace is the most central, best protected part of any Cataphract. It takes hours of work to remove one, and even then it's a difficult, involved process. Moreover, removing an alchemical furnace is … well, noticeable. It would be easier to sabotage a Cataphract's other mechanisms—fray the cables, throw grit into the motive gears, that sort of thing. It'd be less immediate than just breaking things—but that might be the point. Cut a cable here, in the Royal Arsenal, and it's easy to replace. But if you set it up so that a control cable breaks in the field, that creates a far larger problem. It's … well, it's even a problem now, as every machine in the Arsenal is going to have to be checked from toes to helm for sabotage. That takes time."

"That still doesn't tell us who these men are. But I have other ways of finding out. Baron Dunsall and I shall alert the proper authorities. I'm surprised they're not here yet, honestly. You'd think someone would have heard the gunshot." Marquis Maldrinne shook his head. "In the meanwhile, Cousin, I suggest you go back to the *Huntress* and make sure she's ready to march. I'll have men sent to help you stand watch, in case there's more saboteurs lurking about."

"What makes you think I want your help?" Lady Fenvale asked.

"Believe it or not, Cousin, I have bigger goals in life than just making yours miserable," Marquis Maldrinne noted dryly.

"You could have fooled me," Lady Fenvale said.

"I could say the same about you, with what you did at the Summer's Steel festival. But I'm smart enough to know when I've been beaten. You bested me, Countess. You can have that drafty old castle, and you can have the *Huntress*—but now that you've taken your oath, you've got to live up to it. I still don't like you, but I'm willing to put my personal animosity to the side when more important matters are at stake. The question is, are you?"

Lady Fenvale glared at her cousin, seething—but she slowly eased her hand away from where it had unconsciously fallen to the hilt of her saber. "Fine," she grumbled, and held her hand out. "But if this is another trick, I will make you regret it."

Marquis Maldrinne smirked, and shook the offered hand without hesitation.

"How is she?" Lady Fenvale's voice echoed through the *Huntress'* alcove.

"As far as I can tell, she hasn't been touched." Victor held up his oil lantern and ran his fingers over the Cataphract's freshly painted armor, examining closely. He nodded to himself as his theory was confirmed, then went down the scaffolding's narrow stairs, careful not to drop the small lantern. There'd been enough chaos in the Royal Arsenal already. "It's a lucky thing Marissa—Master Smith Chalment and I painted her just a few hours ago. If anyone tried to get at her insides, I'd be able to tell from scratches in the finish." Victor demonstrated by dragging a fingernail over the plating on the *Huntress'* toe, leaving a narrow line on the expanse of otherwise pristine white. "Especially as thin as this paint is."

"Good thinking." Lady Fenvale rubbed at her eyes. Elsewhere in the Royal Arsenal, guards and engineers, rousted from their beds by Marquis Maldrinne, began to rush about, fortifying the building against other intruders.

"I wish I could say that was intentional, but, uh, it was something more of a happy coincidence? First bit of good luck we've had in a while, almost." Victor looked over to where Lily was curled up on a pile of coiled rope, snoring, her muzzle still damp from the cloth Lady Fenvale had used to wipe the pepper dust away. "How is she?"

"She's had worse," Lady Fenvale said. "When she was a pup, she once tried to dig a skunk out of its burrow. It went as well as you'd expect. Poor girl cried for a week after that. Though that was mostly because we made her sleep in the carriage house." Lady Fenvale smiled fondly and crouched down to run her hand over the short brown fur of Lily's coat.

"At least she doesn't smell. Er, that is, at least we don't smell. The dog, that is. Because it wasn't a skunk." Victor set the lantern down on a workbench, then collapsed into a folding chair set up beside it. "You get the idea."

"I do, yes." Lady Fenvale sat down herself, sprawling out next to her dog on the pile of rope, finally letting the day's fatigue catch up with her. Victor wondered when she'd eaten last, only to realize he couldn't remember when *he'd* eaten last. It had been that kind of a day.

Lady Fenvale lolled her head back, leaning against her dog's bulk. "Even if Lily hadn't gotten a snout full of pepper, we don't have time to go chasing all over Kingsforge, not if I'm supposed to march for the North Coast tomorrow. The *Huntress* is ready to march, isn't she?"

"Absolutely." Victor nodded.

"Good." Lady Fenvale closed her eyes and took a deep breath before she sat up straighter. "In the meanwhile, we should talk."

"Oh?"

Lady Fenvale pursed her lips into a line. "Victor Brinden, I release you from my service."

"Wait, what?" The canvas of the folding chair creaked beneath Victor as he sat up straighter. "Have I done something wrong, Countess Fenvale?"

"Quite the opposite," Lady Fenvale said. "You've proven yourself many times over, and you've done the impossible in getting my Cataphract running again. However, given recent events, I don't want you getting hurt on my behalf."

Victor blinked and looked down at his bandaged arm. "I'm afraid it's a bit late for that, Countess."

"Hurt any more, then," Lady Fenvale said, "You're resourceful and industrious. I'm sure you'll have no trouble finding other employment—"

"And if I don't want other employment?" Victor leaned forward, surprising himself with how quickly the question came. "Do you really think I'd be better off working for some lout like Rochen

Dunsall? Or your cousin? Not to mention the practicality of the matter —if you get rid of me, who's going to maintain the *Huntress*? As much as I appreciate your concern for my welfare, I'm just as concerned about yours. I cannot, in good conscience, allow you to throw yourself into danger."

"I can fend for myself, Victor," Lady Fenvale said.

"There's no doubt of that. You are, in fact, somewhat terrifying. But you're no alchemical engineer. Unless you've already lined up someone to replace me, you'll be left without anyone to maintain the *Huntress*, which would be damnably foolish, especially if you're about to go Behemoth hunting. And even if you have found another alchemical engineer you trust to work on your Cataphract, it's going to take time for them to get used to the modifications I've made to the *Huntress'* components and mechanisms. The bellows, for example. Or the link-spars that I had to use to make the *Stalwart*'s motive gears fit correctly, or—"

"Technical details," Lady Fenvale huffed, dismissive.

"Those 'technical details' could easily be the deciding factor of whether you live or die, Countess Fenvale. If I let you charge into battle with an improperly maintained Cataphract, it'd be as bad as sending you into a duel with a dull sword or an empty pistol. So while I appreciate your concern, I cannot, in good conscience, leave you—" Victor blinked, then quickly amended his statement. "—er, which is to say, leave your service."

Lady Fenvale looked down at the saber hanging at her side, as if suddenly considering its sharpness. A long silence hung between them, until she finally stood back up, wincing as she stretched tired muscles. "You make a compelling argument, Chief Engineer Brinden. Now get some sleep—we march in the morning."

CHAPTER 10

Victor strung his hammock up between the *Huntress'* ankles while Lady Fenvale spent the night in the *Huntress'* helm-seat, as if expecting a Behemoth to come climbing over the Lastwall Mountains at any moment. Then again, given his recent luck, Victor supposed that wasn't entirely out of the realm of possibility. A scant few hours later, he woke to the sound of industry.

As soon as the sun rose, the engineers and craftsmen of the Royal Arsenal inspected their war machines from helm to heels to make sure nothing had been damaged or removed during the night. Hammers clanged, winches creaked, and foremen shouted in a rising cacophony of near-panicked industry. A runner arrived, bearing a letter with Marquis Maldrinne's coin-and-dagger seal. Lady Fenvale read it in silence, then refolded it and stuffed it into her doublet. Victor knew better than to ask about the letter's contents, but he supposed it wasn't all bad news, given that Lady Fenvale hadn't immediately started swearing or looking for a sword. Instead, she went out into the mounting chaos of the Royal Arsenal in order to make some last-minute preparations, securing a team of horses for the *Huntress'* supply wagon, along with a quick breakfast: more garlicky sausage buns like they'd had the day before. The very scent of the greasy street food got Lily to drool and wag her tail with barely contained excitement, completely recovered from the previous night's smoke bombing.

Lady Fenvale wolfed her food down even quicker than Lily did and started the climb back up to the *Huntress'* open visor before she finished chewing. She stoked the *Huntress'* furnace and strode out of the Royal Arsenal, while Victor and Lily followed, far less dramatically, in the back of the supply wagon.

The *Huntress* moved smoothly, each complex joint and mechanism working exactly as intended. Victor watched the Cataphract walk and let out a sigh of relief. He hadn't missed any hidden sabotage or other crippling flaw—not yet, at least. With the fresh coat of whitewash, the *Huntress* glowed in the early morning sun, a divine champion machine setting out to protect the weak and helpless, like she had stepped right out of one of those idealized murals on the Royal Palace's ceiling.

Not that anyone seemed to care. The *Huntress'* passing (and reverberating footsteps) attracted onlookers more bleary-eyed than adoring. Victor couldn't fathom how anyone could view something as magnificent as a Cataphract (much less one running as smoothly as the *Huntress*) with annoyance, but there were a lot of things he knew he didn't understand.

At the edge of the city, they met with a small detachment of royal dragoons in full kit, who were to act as the *Huntress'* escort. Lady Fenvale brought the *Huntress* to a stop but left her furnace lit as she opened her visor and slid down a rope.

The dragoons' commander dismounted in turn, moving gracefully despite the polished armor he wore. He tugged off his helmet, revealing a young, handsome face and a mass of long yellow hair that somehow wasn't matted and sweaty yet. Then again, it was still early, Victor mused.

"Lieutenant Julian Iral, at your service." The dragoon bowed deeply. "My men and I await your orders, Countess."

"Glad to hear it." Lady Fenvale bid the lieutenant to stand up straight again. "Lieutenant, this is Chief Engineer Brinden, my second-in-command. If, for whatever reason, I am unavailable, you are to report to him. Understood?"

"Of course, Countess." Lieutenant Iral's smile didn't falter as he nodded to Victor. "I'll look forward to working with you."

"Likewise?" Victor tried not to buckle under the sudden and unexpected responsibility Lady Fenvale had foisted on him. He turned his head to give the countess a questioning look, but she didn't notice.

"Forgive me for the brief introduction, Lieutenant, but we haven't any time to waste on pleasantries. I trust your men are ready to ride?"

"Of course, Countess." The young officer stood up straighter.

"Good. Send four of your men to scout ahead, and have them report back with anything out of the ordinary."

"Already?" Lieutenant Iral blinked. "We're not even through Northpass yet. Surely if there was any threat—"

"We're not going to let it take us by surprise," Lady Fenvale said, stern. "If nothing else, consider it practice. I want to see how well your men can ride, Lieutenant. Impress me."

"Understood, Countess!" Lieutenant Iral replied, then turned to bark orders at his men. Four of the dragoons turned their horses and galloped down the road to scout ahead. The rest formed up in rows on either side of the *Huntress*.

Lady Fenvale took in the dragoons' parade ground precision, then nodded in approval. "I was almost afraid my cousin would try to saddle me with a bunch of useless layabouts."

"Perish the thought, Countess," Lieutenant Iral said. "I volunteered for this assignment, as did every one of my men. It's not every day one gets to serve a Beasthunter-Errant."

"And it's not every day one gets to hunt a Behemoth, either," Lady Fenvale said with a faint, grim smile. "Which is why we'll need to move quickly. Do try to keep up." With that, Lady Fenvale went back to the *Huntress*. Lieutenant Iral lingered in place and watched the countess haul herself up into her Cataphract's helm-seat. A fresh cloud of smoke plumed from the machine's exhaust vents as Lady Fenvale prepared to march once more.

"Magnificent," Lieutenant Iral marveled.

"The *Huntress* is an impressive machine, yes." Victor smiled with pride to see the Cataphract working so well, then turned to head back to his place on the supply wagon.

"With a fittingly impressive captain, no less." Lieutenant Iral didn't return to his horse, but fell into step beside Victor instead. "You know the countess well, don't you?"

"I—" Victor considered the matter. "I suppose so? Better than most, at least."

"Perfect!" Lieutenant Iral smiled a dazzling smile and clapped Victor on the arm. "I'm sure there's much you can tell me about Countess Fenvale."

"Is there?" Victor glanced up at the *Huntress* as Lady Fenvale started working the controls. "I mean, Countess Fenvale is fairly … straightforward in her disposition. Refreshingly so, in that respect. If you make her mad, she'll let you know." Victor stepped out of the way as Lily bounded into the back of the supply wagon and immediately flopped down on a canvas-wrapped bundle.

"Direct, hm?" Lieutenant Iral rubbed at his clean-shaven chin in a vague approximation of thoughtfulness. "Then perhaps I'll just ask the countess to marry me right away."

"Marry you?" Victor blurted.

"Don't look so shocked!" The dashing dragoon drew himself up taller and tossed his long blond hair back in a gesture entirely too casual to not have been rehearsed. "My family may not own a Cataphract as the Fenvales do, but I come from respectable stock. Quite a suitable match for a Beasthunter-Errant, I dare say."

"That's not why you volunteered, was it? To get close to Countess Fenvale so you could … woo her?" Victor chose his words carefully, as if he were guiding someone away from a steep cliff, or a particularly volatile experiment.

"Of course not!" Lieutenant Iral said. "I volunteered because this sounded like the most interesting assignment to come along in ages. To hunt a Behemoth, like something out of a Summer's-Steel play? How could I resist? It's either fame and adventure and glory— or, if the whole thing is a hoax, I'll get to spend time with a most striking young lady. Does Countess Fenvale like sonnets? I've been meaning to learn how to write sonnets."

"I wouldn't," Victor said. "Learn how to write sonnets, that is. Or at least not solely for Countess Fenvale's sake."

"She's not much for poetry, then?"

"She's not much for anything. The countess is already spoken for." Victor thought back to how they'd left Rosalind Manor. "I think. Best not to get involved, either way."

"So the countess already has a paramour? I should have figured. Who's the lucky gentleman?" asked Lieutenant Iral.

"I'm not at liberty to say."

Lieutenant Iral leaned forward, examining Victor. "Wait, it's not you, is it?"

Despite his fatigue, Victor broke out laughing. "Ah, no. Not me. I am most assuredly not the sort of man to garner Countess Fenvale's affection. And neither are you, for that matter. We'll all have a lot more to worry about once we get to the North Coast and start tracking down this Behemoth."

"Hah!" Lieutenant Iral's laugh came cheery and guileless. "You've got a point there. I suppose if the countess won't be interested in the likes of me, that just means we should hope we'll get to chase a monster after all, hm? Why, if I return to the capital with a suitably impressive trophy, I'll be up to my armpits in baronesses and duchesses. All the -esses a man could want! Ha!"

Victor shook his head as he climbed into the supply wagon. "One thing at a time, Lieutenant. It's best not to get ahead of ourselves."

Over the next few days, Lady Fenvale kept the *Huntress* in near-constant motion, setting out shortly after dawn and only stopping when the sun was barely a handspan above the western horizon. Sometimes they stayed at the grand houses set up along the Cataphract road to enjoy the local lord's hospitality; Lady Fenvale made it a point to get underway even earlier on those days, prompting vaguely hungover grumbling from the dragoons. Even still, Lady Fenvale glared the cavalrymen into submission, and everyone got into the routine of travel as they pressed northward as fast as could be managed.

As the miles went on, the *Huntress'* whitewash began to fade and peel away, to the point where Victor could calculate a rough approximation of how far they'd traveled by how much paint had flaked from the armor plating. At least, he could until the rain started, and the last of the thin paint melted to reveal the plain metal beneath.

They marched through the Northpass, around the dense oaks surrounding Lake Nim, and finally into the rocks and crags and general grayness of the North Coast. It took them seventeen days of hard travel to get there, slower than Duke Astello's mad ride, but still a quite respectable pace for a fully equipped Cataphract and escort. Even before the ocean came into view, Victor smelled salt on the cool wind and immediately started to worry about how the salty air and near-constant rain would affect the *Huntress'* inner workings. He hoped they'd be done Behemoth hunting before rust became too much of an issue, but double-checked his supply of gear grease nonetheless.

It was raining when they made it to Braveharbor. Then again, it had rained every day for the prior week, long enough for Victor to forget what dry socks felt like.

The city (the only one of consequence along the North Coast) was so named for the fact that it took a brave man to live there, back when Behemoths were said to drag themselves from the depths of the ocean every time the moon was full. Life in Braveharbor had settled down in the intervening centuries as the city grew fat on fishing and commerce, but Braveharbor's name had stuck. The city was built up around a crescent-shaped bay that offered protection to the various fishermen and trading vessels clustered inside. At a glance, everything looked peaceful. No enormous beasts rose up on the horizon, and no streams of panicked refugees clogged the road. It wasn't entirely peaceful, however. A duelist-class Cataphract stood before the city's main gate, standing watch over the road: the *Major Simon*, Victor presumed. Thin trails of smoke rose from her exhaust vents, showing

Major Simon's captain took his watch duty seriously, ready to spring into action if needed.

The *Major Simon* raised her lance in salute as the *Huntress* approached, and Lady Fenvale returned the gesture. This done, the two stepped aside, and the *Major Simon* even swept one hand out in a gallant gesture for Lady Fenvale to pass through Braveharbor's open gate. Her visor hinged open, and her captain stood up in his helm-seat, mirroring his Cataphract's gesture as he swept his hat off in a bow.

"Welcome to Braveharbor!" *Major Simon*'s captain called out through a speaking cone. "Prince Edval is expecting you at his castle. We sent word ahead as soon as we saw you coming."

Lady Fenvale lowered the *Huntress'* sword and rested it against her shoulder as she obligingly walked into the city, dragoons and supply wagon following. As they went through the streets of Braveharbor, Victor noticed small clues, signs of something amiss. Despite the early afternoon hour, the streets were oddly quiet and sedate, mostly clear of the bustle and business one would expect from a port city. The streets were empty, and the various storefronts and food stalls were closed. Looking down at the city's namesake harbor, Victor saw the reason why. No vessels went in or out of the harbor; instead, the boats were packed tight around the docks, sails furled.

Prince Edval's castle stood at one of the points of the harbor's crescent, standing watch over the bay. It was a towering, ancient structure, unquestionably a fortress first and a royal dwelling second. There was only one approach to the castle, a long, narrow path currently guarded by the *Tender Mercy of Queen Jeriel*. The hulking siegebreaker's silhouette matched the blocky architecture of the castle, as if the fortress and its guardian had been built as a matched set. Given that the *Queen Jeriel* was the personal property of Prince Edval himself, this might have been the case. The *Tender Mercy of Queen Jeriel* carried a war hammer the size of a lighthouse, capable of crushing city walls or smaller Cataphracts in a single blow. No smoke came from her vents, Victor noted. The huge Cataphract was powered down but still intimidating nonetheless.

The *Huntress* lowered herself on one knee and opened her visor. Lady Fenvale tossed out a rope ladder and climbed down.

Protected from the elements by the *Huntress'* visor, she was fortunate enough to remain mostly dry and mostly presentable after the day's march. Behind her, the dragoons and supply wagon came to a halt in the open plaza in front of the castle. Lily hopped out of the wagon with a nimbleness one wouldn't expect from a creature so big, and Victor followed suit (albeit with far less spring in his step). The dragoons dismounted, laughing and joking amongst themselves as they stretched their journey-stiffened legs.

"Victor, Lieutenant, with me." Lady Fenvale waved them over. "Lily, stay," she ordered the dog, who gave a faint whine of protest but went over to shelter from the rain beneath the *Huntress*. With her Cataphract so guarded, Lady Fenvale walked up the stairs to the castle's main door. A jowly old man in ruffles and finery stood just inside, out of the rain. He appraised them, not bothering to hide his distaste before he finally rapped his chamberlain's staff against the ground and gestured for the heavy doors to open.

"Prince Edval awaits."

By Victor's reckoning, Braveharbor Castle was remarkably unremarkable. The architecture was large and imposing, true—but at the same time it lacked the ornate grandeur of the Royal Palace at Kingsforge, or the conspicuous opulence of Maldrinne House. It was as if the palace architecture was meant to remind Prince Edval of his secondary role in the royal hierarchy. Perhaps it was, Victor mused; that seemed like the sort of calculated pettiness that the aristocracy thrived on. The "second best" nature followed through to Prince Edval himself; though he was taller than the king, he was also slimmer of build, near the point of sickliness. He wore the trappings of a man of his station: lace ruffles, a fortune's worth of jewels, and a complicated coiffure of black curls that may or may not have been a wig. Instead of making Prince Edval look more regal, however, the piled-on finery made him look smaller, like a man dredged from the ruins of a recently exploded wardrobe.

Prince Edval received them in the main gallery, itself a smaller, less impressive imitation of the Hall of the Forge-Throne. He sat on a tall, high-backed chair—albeit one that probably didn't hide any secret passages to underground labyrinths. To judge by the expression on Prince Edval's face, it wasn't a particularly comfortable seat, either.

The prince took in the sight of Lady Fenvale and her entourage and drummed his fingers on the arm of his chair. Lady Fenvale stood straight-backed and silent, as cool as if she'd been facing down a squadron of enemy Cataphracts. Victor tried to match her confidence, with little success. Lucky for Victor, Prince Edval focused more on the countess, regarding her in the way a spoiled child might look at steamed vegetables suddenly dropped on his plate in place of dessert. The various fops and courtiers present all mirrored the prince's expression.

Finally, Prince Edval spoke.

"I ask for help, and my brother sends a woman."

"You asked the king for help, and His Majesty has sent the Beasthunter-Errant." Lady Fenvale tilted her chin up, defiant. She met Prince Edval's appraising look with one of her own, and made no attempt to hide the fact that she found him lacking. A murmur rippled through Prince Edval's court, the sort of visibly spreading rumor that Victor had come to recognize as something of an inevitability whenever Lady Fenvale went to a social function. However, this time, Lady Fenvale had more than just a large dog and a sharp saber backing her. She pulled her letter of commission out of her maroon tunic and held it out. "My credentials, Your Highness."

Prince Edval nodded to his chamberlain, and the older man scuttled forward to examine the document. He fished a monocle from his waistcoat and held it to his eye as he squinted at the royal seals and signatures. After concluding the letter to be official and genuine, the chamberlain turned and nodded to Prince Edval. "Her documents are in order, sire." He sounded mildly disappointed to say it.

"Do check again, Chamberlain Bouslet." Prince Edval still looked skeptical. "I was unaware the kingdom had a Beasthunter-Errant."

Lady Fenvale shrugged. "And I was unaware Braveharbor had a Behemoth problem, sir."

"An alleged Behemoth," said the prince. "My son was … rash, in bringing this to the Crown's attention. As you can see, we are not under threat."

"Yet you've called up every Cataphract in the region," Lady Fenvale noted.

"To comfort my people." Prince Edval waved airily, gesturing to the court—and, by extension, Braveharbor. "Unfortunately, not everyone is as enlightened or educated as I am. Once word got out that someone had sighted a Behemoth, I had to take steps to prevent panic and chaos. I'm less concerned with some theoretical monster, and more with those that might try to take advantage of the situation. Thankfully, the mere presence of my loyal captains has been enough to keep the peace. Even still, I'm sure they shall be pleased to have the *Huntress*' assistance. My captains will draw up a schedule for you— having another duelist to act on sentry duty shall prove quite useful, I'm sure. The *Huntress* will stand watch over the main road while the other Cataphracts—"

"Sir," Lady Fenvale said flatly. "That isn't why I was sent here."

Prince Edval steepled his fingers. "You came to protect the people of the Northcoast, did you not?"

"I came to hunt Behemoths. And I cannot do that if the *Huntress* is relegated to sentry duty."

Prince Edval scowled in the manner of someone not used to hearing the word "no." "And how do you expect to hunt, Countess? Is your engineer so brilliant that he's gotten the *Huntress* to swim?"

At the prince's pointed jest, Chamberlain Bouslet and the rest of the courtiers obediently provided a subdued, but no less mocking laugh. Victor forced a smile, even though he hadn't been officially introduced as Lady Fenvale's engineer. Between his glasses, the grease beneath his fingernails, and general nebbish air, Victor's profession was obvious to anyone who'd care to notice. As Victor endured the mocking laughter, a spark of inquiry flickered at the back of his mind. Why couldn't a Cataphract be designed to swim? They were designed to move and fight like a man could—and men could swim. Some of them, at least. The first thing would be to seal all the Cataphract's workings so they didn't flood the moment she went into the water. Perhaps a "skin" of oiled leather could protect the gears and furnaces—

Lady Fenvale's reply snapped Victor out of his brainstorming. "As it would happen, Chief Engineer Brinden is brilliant—but going out to sea wasn't my plan. I intend to conduct my hunt like a proper campaign, Prince Edval. Starting with a good map and whatever information you have about these Behemoth sightings. Time, location, heading—based on that, I may be able to predict where the Behemoth will strike, and make preparations accordingly."

"And how do you prepare for something like a Behemoth?" Prince Edval sneered. "Provided one even exists, which still hasn't been proven."

"We can post lookouts and messengers along the coast and have them send word if they see a Behemoth approaching. With four Cataphracts, we could post them—"

"I beg your pardon, Countess," Prince Edval cut in. "Did you say four Cataphracts? I was unaware you'd brought such a squadron with you."

Lady Fenvale blinked. "I didn't. But between the *Huntress*, the *Challenge*, the *Major Simon*, and The *Tender Mercy of Queen Jeriel*, we should be able to cover a large stretch of—"

"Such insolence!" Prince Edval shouted as he jumped to his feet. The sudden burst of movement was enough to make even Lady Fenvale step back in surprise. The prince's cheeks flushed red, visible even beneath his layers of white powder. He jabbed an accusatory finger at Lady Fenvale, which would've been a more intimidating gesture if his hand wasn't surrounded by the lace cloud spilling out of his cuff. "First you refuse to serve me, now you presume to tell me how to best use the Cataphracts under my command? If it weren't for the letter of commission you convinced my brother to give you, I'd have you arrested and your *Huntress* put to better use."

The faint clink of steel echoed through the room as hands crept towards swords.

"You could try, Prince Edval." Lady Fenvale gritted her teeth and leveled her icy glare at the prince's men, a silent promise that she would not go easy, if things came to it. "But I know you won't. You're far too loyal a brother to do anything that could be interpreted … unkindly. Especially with your own son still enjoying His Majesty's hospitality at Kingsforge."

Prince Edval glared at Lady Fenvale, fuming, and finally shook his head. "So be it." He eased himself back onto his throne, then turned to his chamberlain. "You may have whatever papers you require, Countess, and you may talk to as many superstitious idiots as you like, for whatever good that may do you. But I will not lend you the use of a single pikeman, to say nothing of my Cataphracts. Braveharbor cannot be left undefended in this time of crisis. Now, remove yourself from my sight, Beasthunter." The prince sneered.

"Thank you, Your Highness." Lady Fenvale bared her teeth in a polite snarl of a smile and bowed only as far as she had to. "I shall remember this meeting."

Prince Edval didn't bother looking at Lady Fenvale, instead coolly examining the glint of light off one of his jeweled rings. "See that you do."

After Prince Edval's dismissal, Lady Fenvale found Chamberlain Bouslet and intimidated the harried-looking man into leading her to his office. There, she loaded up on maps, charts, logbooks, and other official-looking documentation, scooping things up seemingly at random. She foisted a heavy valise onto Victor, and then remained quiet until the two of them were descending the castle steps.

"That could have gone better," Lady Fenvale muttered. The *Huntress* was right where they had left it: kneeling on the other side of the plaza, across from the *Tender Mercy of Queen Jeriel*.

"It could have gone worse?" Victor offered. "I mean, you didn't even have to draw your sword."

"That's a low bar to set, Victor." Lady Fenvale blew a long breath out through her mouth. "I thought captaining the *Huntress* would free me from all the useless ceremony and idiotic posturing. Free me from the politics. I came here to fight a damned monster, and the first thing I do is start arguing with the king's brother."

Victor and Lady Fenvale both relaxed once they stood in the *Huntress'* shadow once more; after the last few months, they had both come to find the machine's presence somewhat comforting, one of the few constants to be had in the last several weeks they'd spent traveling from one end of the kingdom to the next. Lily wagged her tail as they approached.

"To be fair, he started it." Victor tried for optimism. "You handled it rather well, if you ask me."

"I handled it like my cousin would." Lady Fenvale rubbed at the bridge of her nose, as if the admission physically pained her.

"Something tells me Marquis Maldrinne would be a little more subtle," Victor said, though the words sounded far more reassuring in his head.

Lady Fenvale scowled at Victor, only to break into a rueful laugh a moment later. "You may be right. He'd just bribe the prince and blackmail the Behemoth."

"Or the other way around," Victor said, and started laughing himself.

"Looks like we'll just have to do things the hard way." Lady Fenvale shook her head, and a few loose strands of dark hair bobbed around her face. "We've got several hundred miles of coastline to defend with little more than a single Cataphract, a handful of light cavalry, and Lily here." She ran her hand over the bristly fur on the big dog's back, and Lily's mouth hung open in a happy canine smile.

"Given what we've been through so far, I'd say that's more than enough." The false bravado hung off Victor like an ill-fitting coat.

Lady Fenvale smiled anyway. "I hope you're right."

Victor glanced back at the castle. "Did you really expect the prince to help?"

"Honestly? Yes. More fool me, to think that the king's brother would raise a finger in defense of his own people. Bah." Lady Fenvale spat on the rain-slicked cobblestones.

"Assuming, of course, there's something to actually defend them from," Victor said.

Lady Fenvale shook her head again. "It's not a hoax," she said decisively.

"You're sure?"

"I've been sure ever since we were ambushed at the Royal Arsenal. Whether or not the Behemoths have returned, something is going on. Honestly, I'm kind of surprised no one else has tried to kill us yet." Lady Fenvale's left hand unconsciously came to rest on the pommel of her saber as she spoke.

"You sound disappointed," Victor said, only half joking.

"At least we'd know who our enemies were," Lady Fenvale muttered.

"I'm not sure if that's true," Victor said. "We still don't know who attacked us at the Royal Arsenal. Though your cousin, for all his flaws, is clever. Conniving, even. Something tells me he's just the man to uncover who those saboteurs were working for."

"You may be right, Victor. But my cousin will only tell us what he's learned if he thinks it'll benefit him somehow." She shook her head. "There's no use worrying about it. Best we focus on the matter at hand. We've got to learn everything we can about these Behemoth sightings if we're going to do anything about them. Fortunately, I at least know how to take care of that."

"You do? Where do we start?"

"First thing, we buy a drink."

CHAPTER 11

The Bell and Kettle sat along a thoroughfare not far from Braveharbor's main gate. Lady Fenvale picked the inn for its location, and also for the stable yard behind it that just had enough room for the *Huntress* to kneel down without crushing anything too important.

Under the countess' orders, Lieutenant Iral and his men spread out through the city to gather information—and also to spread it. The dragoons went out in pairs, making a circuit of Braveharbor's dockside taverns and wineshops in search of anyone who might have seen the Behemoth out at sea, with word that the king had sent the Beasthunter-Errant to track down the monster, and that said Beasthunter-Errant would, for one night, buy a tall beer for anyone with reliable information on the creature. Two of them, if she liked your story.

In a matter of hours, a long line of thirsty would-be storytellers queued up outside. Lady Fenvale transformed the first floor of the inn into a vague approximation of a noble's court: she sat in a creaky, wicker-backed chair, while Victor sat to her left, scribbling down notes (Lily, meanwhile, found a more comfortable spot curled up near the hearth). Lieutenant Iral and a handful of his dragoons stood near the door, ostensibly standing guard.

They received the witnesses one at a time, listening to their stories from the other end of a beer-stained, knife-marked table. Most of the stories were rambling and incoherent (the free beer likely didn't help much in that respect), but Lady Fenvale subtly directed the conversation in more productive directions. She asked pointed questions, seeking out specific details like dates, times, weather conditions, and the name of the ship they happened to be on. Other details were harder to come by. Some said the Behemoth was twice as long as a sailing ship, while other sailors swore it was no bigger than a rowboat. Depending on who one asked, the Behemoth had the fins of a whale, the teeth of a shark, the tentacles of a squid, or some horrid combination thereof. One sunbaked old codger had a different take.

"It were a woman! A giantess, tall as a siegebreaker! Skin the color of honey, and with all of it out for anybody to see! Bosoms as big as—"

"That will be all, thank you," Lady Fenvale said curtly. She cleared her throat, and Lieutenant Iral gently but firmly showed the man out. Once he did, Lady Fenvale slumped in her chair. "I think that's enough for the night, Lieutenant. Inform anyone still waiting outside that we'll get to them tomorrow, then lock the door."

"Understood, Countess." The lieutenant snapped his fingers, and two of his dragoons followed him outside to relay the news.

Lady Fenvale took a long pull from a mug of dark beer, wiped her mouth with the back of her hand, and then stood up to stretch. "What do we have, Victor? Anything useful?"

"Right now, we have sixty-eight eyewitness accounts, of … varying reliability." The engineer flexed his ink-blacked fingers, trying to dispel a cramp that had come from clutching his pen for hours. "The good news is, the accounts of the first Behemoth sighting seem to corroborate each other. Furthermore, based on the information we have, I think we can confirm at least four, maybe five other sightings. On the other hand, the majority of the stories are likely outright fabrications. Like that last one, for example."

"You don't think the Behemoth will take the form of an enormous naked woman?" Lady Fenvale said, deadpan.

"I, er, find it highly unlikely, yes." Victor started shuffling through his notes. "Still, I think we've gotten more good information than bad. I just hope it's worth it. I also kept a running count of how much beer we gave away. It's a … considerable amount, even before we get into what we drank ourselves. I trust you've made arrangements with the innkeeper?"

"That, at least, we don't have to worry about." Lady Fenvale grinned, then started rummaging through the valise of documents they'd got from Prince Edval's chamberlain. "When I was getting the maps, I made it a point to pick up a few writs of acquisition as well." She pulled out one such document, properly sealed and signed, a guarantee that Prince Edval would cover any debts that might be accrued in service to the kingdom. "The prince may have refused to lend me his Cataphracts, but he did promise to give me any document I might need," she noted with a sly smirk.

"And the chamberlain just … gave those to you?"

"They might have gotten mixed up in the hustle and bustle," Lady Fenvale said with a little shrug.

"Is that, er—legal?"

"Legal enough." Lady Fenvale shrugged. "Besides, if Prince Edval can't cover our bar tab, then he's got bigger problems to worry about. As do we." She set the writ of acquisition aside and slid a paper map out of a long tubular carrying case. She spread the map out on the table in front of them and pinned the corners down with empty bottles (which they had in ready supply). On the thick, yellowed paper, the North Coast stretched out before them, a jagged line of cliffs and peninsulas and the occasional small island. Lady Fenvale traced a finger over the map, then stopped on an expanse of empty sea. "The first sighting was here, yes?"

"In the general vicinity, yes. But I think I can get more specific than that." Victor took drafting tools out of a leather case, then leaned in to pore over the map. He double-checked his notes, and then, with the use of a compass, he very carefully drew a small circle on the map, close to where Lady Fenvale's finger had pointed. "Based on the accounts we have, the first Behemoth sighting was somewhere within this area. Which, admittedly, was quite some time ago, so it seems unlikely that the Behemoth will be in the same place. It could be hundreds of miles away by now. Unless, say, it has some sort of underwater nest that it's lurking in. But that's something of a moot point, since the *Huntress* can't swim."

"Any idea on why it hasn't made landfall?"

Victor tapped a finger on the hinged end of his drafting compass. "I don't know. It's entirely possible that the Behemoth could

111

be entirely aquatic, in which case it can't make landfall, any more than a trout can walk. Alternately, it might be waiting for something."

"For what?" Lady Fenvale asked.

"Changes in the weather, or the tides, phases of the moon, or perhaps some other variable that we're not even aware of. However, we may be able to narrow things down if we factor in some of the other accounts." He shuffled through his notes and leaned in close to verify the details. Carefully, he drew another circle on the map, some distance from the first. He repeated the process, and then again a third time, meticulously marking points based on the most reliable accounts they'd just received. He penciled in the date and time of each sighting inside each circle, along with a number to indicate which account the information came from. Victor sketched in a half dozen of the most reliable reports and then took a step back to survey his handiwork. "I don't see a pattern. Not yet, at least, but we can still extrapolate some information from what we have so far. For example—" Victor took a straight edge and drew a thin line between two of the circles. "These two sightings were only three days apart. Which means we can calculate how far the Behemoth can move in a day. Or at least get a rough estimate. I honestly wouldn't be surprised if it could move far faster if it wanted to."

Lady Fenvale tapped a finger on the scratched brass handguard of the sword at her side. "Assuming there's only one Behemoth."

"Er, yes," Victor said. "It's not impossible that this Behemoth could have a mate, or perhaps even spawn of its own. But I think it's unlikely. Each sighting has been of just one creature, the same creature, if we go by the most reliable accounts."

"What about the unreliable ones?" Lady Fenvale leaned past Victor and picked up his notebook, leafing through curiously.

"That's going to be the most challenging part, sorting the wheat from the chaff."

"Don't." She put Victor's open notebook on the table, then went back to the other papers they'd received from the chamberlain. Victor winced as she piled various documents onto an empty (but not entirely dry) corner of the table until she found what she was looking for: a registry of trade ships and fishing boats. She plopped the leather-bound registry next to Victor's notes and started looking between them. "Even if half those sailors were lying—"

"The ratio may be closer to two-thirds," Victor noted with an embarrassed wince.

Lady Fenvale pressed on. "They have to be from somewhere."

Victor blinked. "How do you mean?"

"Every man we just bought beer for saw the Behemoth while they were at sea. What we have here," she patted the registry, "is an account of every ship in the harbor, and where those ships came from. Even that old coot going on about giant mermaid tits had to be onboard one of the vessels recorded here." She looked between Victor's notes and the ship registry, cross-referencing the information. "And here it is. A fishing boat called the ... Leaky Lecher."

"That's, er, appropriate? Or, well, appropriately inappropriate, given his story." Victor managed a nervous smile. "But I don't see how that helps?"

"This registry says the Leaky Lecher isn't from Braveharbor. Instead, it's coming from a little town called Urchin Rock, which is ... " Lady Fenvale leaned over the map again, dark eyes scanning the coastline until she found what she was looking for. "Here." She picked up a pencil and scribbled a rough "x" beside the town's name on the map.

"And?"

"Even if the man's full of it, which he obviously is, the fact that his ship made it here intact tells us something: where the Behemoth isn't, at the very least." She nodded, resolute. "Victor, I want you to find out where each ship on our list came from and mark its home port on the map. At least the ships that came from elsewhere on the North Coast. Can you do that?"

"I can, yes," Victor said. "But don't you think we should focus on the more credible accounts?"

"Not yet," Lady Fenvale mused. "Especially since we don't know enough to really decide what's credible and what isn't. I'm going to check in with Lieutenant Iral—we'll review your findings once I get back."

"My findings? I'm not exactly sure what I'm looking for to begin with."

"Just mark the map, Victor. The rest will come together in due time."

Lady Fenvale picked up her hat, Victor picked up a pencil, and both of them got to work.

The research wasn't hard, merely tedious. The registry of ships' names wasn't organized to Victor's liking, and it wasn't as if the little villages and hamlets along the North Coast were laid out in alphabetical order, either. Once he located the home port of each boat, Victor marked it on the map and wrote down the name of the vessel hailing from there. Thankfully, sixty-eight different witnesses didn't mean sixty-eight different ships; many of the sailors served on the same ship and thus shared the same home port. By the time Victor had the map covered with notes, his eyes ached and his fingers cramped. He deliberately set down his pencil, took off his glasses, and pressed his palms over his eyes to rub the dryness away.

"Here." Lady Fenvale walked over from the bar and set something on the table in front of Victor. He opened bleary eyes and looked down at a mug of oak-brown beer. "It'll help," she said.

"Thank you." Victor slouched in his chair and glanced around the inn's common room. It was dark outside, the fire had burned down to coals, and the glass oil lamps hanging from the ceiling sputtered with the last licks of tallow oil. No wonder his eyes hurt. Victor fumbled his glasses back on and looked down at the tangle of lines and notes stretching across the map ahead of him, their details made fuzzy by the scant light. "I've marked the boats' points of origin—or, well,

114

those with points of origin to mark. One of the trade ships hails from the Silkmaker Isles, so obviously its home port isn't on any of the maps we've acquired. Still, if you give me another hour or two, I can —" Victor stifled a yawn, then shook his head. "I can corroborate the most accurate accounts and make some predictions as to where the Behemoth may be headed." He reached for his pencil again.

Lady Fenvale laid a hand over his. "Wait."

"I appreciate the concern, Lady Fenvale, but I'm used to working late hours—"

"Finish it tomorrow." The countess unhooked one of the hanging oil lamps and carefully set it down on the table to illuminate a particular stretch of the map. "You've already given me something to work with. Look." She pointed to a blank stretch of coast on the map, one of the few points that didn't have an X marked nearby to mark it as the home port of one fishing boat or another.

Victor picked up his beer instead of his pencil and squinted at the spot on the map Lady Fenvale pointed to. "It's just another fishing village, albeit one we haven't heard from."

"Exactly." Lady Fenvale's hunter's smile shone white and sharp in the dim light. "That's what we're looking for."

"I don't follow," Victor said.

The countess pulled up a chair and sat down. "Have you ever hunted wolves, Victor?"

"I think it's fairly obvious I haven't."

"Out in the forest, you'll never hear a wolf, not when it's close. Instead, you have to listen for the absence of sound. Birds stop singing when a wolf is near. Sometimes, that's the only warning you get that the wolf is hunting you."

"These are people, not songbirds." Victor furrowed his brow. "It could be that they've just been lucky enough to avoid the Behemoth."

"Or unlucky enough to be at the center of all this." Lady Fenvale tapped an impatient finger on the pommel of her saber. "Either way, I intend to find out."

CHAPTER 12

The village was named Clam-Rake, and certainly looked the part.

Hardly more than a collection of damp and drafty-looking cottages, the village sat at the end of a narrow inlet, four days' overland march from Braveharbor. With the right wind, a ship could travel the same distance in a quarter of the time. Which made it all the more odd that no one from Clam-Rake had been to Braveharbor in the last several weeks, Victor realized.

From her perch atop the *Huntress*, Lady Fenvale squinted through a spyglass, taking in the sight of the sleepy, quiet village. Between the *Huntress'* stature and the hill the Cataphract stood on, she had a perfect view of the small coastal village. A chill, salty breeze blew over the hilltop, causing Lady Fenvale's hair and coat to flicker behind her. She scanned the area for several minutes before descending to join Lily and Victor on the ground. Lieutenant Iral and his dragoons stood a short distance behind them, still on horseback, milling around the supply wagon.

"It's quiet," Lady Fenvale said. "Like every other little village we passed on the way here."

"May I take a look?" Victor asked, and Lady Fenvale obligingly handed him the spyglass. He held the telescope up to his right eye and peered through it. Tiny figures, wrapped in gray wool shawls to protect from the afternoon's drizzle, shuffled about in pairs and trios. They went from one ramshackle building to the next, back and forth across the small common area in the center of the village, working on whatever chores were needed around a tiny fishing hamlet. A handful of fishing boats sat moored to the docks; Victor wished he knew enough about fishing to determine whether that was normal or not. He pursed his lips, looking for anything else that might be out of the ordinary, and soon found it. "That's odd."

"What is?" Lady Fenvale asked.

Without being asked, Victor handed the spyglass back to the countess. "Look at all the cargo they've got stowed by the docks. I can't tell what it is with canvas draped over it, but it seems a bit … excessive, given where we are." He bit the inside of his cheek and ran some rough calculations in his head. "In fact, I daresay it's more cargo than any one of those little fishing boats could handle."

"Smugglers, then?" Lady Fenvale asked without turning her head.

"That might explain why they haven't sent anyone to Braveharbor." Victor rubbed at his chin. "With everyone on edge because of a Behemoth, they might be afraid to draw more attention."

"Or they could be using the rumors as an opportunity to move their cargo without anyone noticing." Lady Fenvale tracked the lens of her spyglass across the fishing village, searching for more clues. "Or it could be—shit!" Her eyes went wide behind the eyepiece, and her cheeks went pale.

Victor started at the sudden exclamation, and Lily let out a nervous whine. "What is it?"

Lady Fenvale tossed the spyglass into Victor's fumbling hands and leapt for the *Huntress'* leg, scrambling upwards. "It's the Behemoth!"

Barely managing not to drop the telescope, Victor once again turned his attention to the village. Sure enough, an enormous something rose up through the water at the mouth of the narrow bay, churning through the otherwise-placid water. Even at that distance, Victor could tell the Behemoth was obviously bigger than the *Huntress*, bigger than a siegebreaker, bigger than any man-made object for miles around. The huge monster looked like nothing Victor had ever seen or studied, but given the dearth of information on the ancient beasts, that wasn't surprising. It had the appearance of an enormous fish, hybridized with some sort of deep-sea crustacean. Seawater coursed off the creature's curved, greenish carapace as it surfaced, and light shone from its glassy, bulbous eyes. Absurdly, Victor realized how, from the right angle (and possibly after a large amount of rum), someone might see the Behemoth's curved shell as vaguely feminine.

He kept that information to himself.

"Lieutenant!" Lady Fenvale vaulted into the *Huntress'* open visor. "Take half your men and ride for Braveharbor, and send the other half the other way along the coast to warn the next village over. Go!"

"At once, Countess. Happy hunting!" The lieutenant saluted, then started shouting orders at the other dragoons, who quickly wheeled their horses around and took off at a gallop.

"Victor, you and Lily stay with the supply wagon," Lady Fenvale shouted down at them as she started working the *Huntress'* control levers.

"You're going to fight it?" With Lily at his heels, Victor dashed out to the side so as not to get crushed beneath the Cataphract's massive feet. "Now?"

"I may not get another chance." Lady Fenvale closed the *Huntress'* visor with a heavy, metallic clank and pushed the war machine into motion. Her heavy footfalls shook the ground, building up speed and momentum as she strode down the slope towards Clam-Rake, and the monster swimming up the cove. The *Huntress* shifted her broadsword from where it rested on her shoulder, holding the hilt with both hands in preparation of the coming melee. The *Huntress* was running smoothly, perhaps better than she had in years—Victor hoped it would be enough.

Meanwhile, the Behemoth continued its steady, almost leisurely swim through the inlet, bearing down on the village. As the *Huntress* and the sea monster got closer and closer, the knot in Victor's stomach only grew tighter and tighter. With a sudden, terrible epiphany, Victor realized just what was wrong, the proverbial songbirds going quiet in a wolf's presence.

The villagers weren't running.

Squinting through the telescope, Victor watched a half dozen fishermen dash towards the docks, as if to greet the approaching beast. Had they domesticated the Behemoth, somehow? Or had they come to worship it as some sort of pagan god-beast? There were dozens of tales where superstitious villagers would try to placate the ravenous monsters with human sacrifices, only for a passing hero to save the day. How much truth was there to the old stories? And how far would these fishermen go to defend their Behemoth? More questions roiled through Victor's mind as he watched, helpless, already too far away to warn Lady Fenvale.

The *Huntress* stormed into the village of Clam-Rake, sword leveled at the Behemoth like a knight's jousting lance, ready to put literal tons of force behind a single, stabbing thrust. Heedless of the danger, the Behemoth drifted to a halt beside the dock, and several villagers jumped onto the monster's shell. Victor could only wonder if they were trying to get out of the *Huntress'* way, or if they were trying to warn the beast. Had they prepared any other tricks or defenses?

Too late, Victor found out.

So focused on her headlong charge, there was no way Lady Fenvale could have seen the thick anchor chain draped across the single dirt road leading into the village. Nor could she see the complicated array of pulleys and weights attached to either end of the chain, or the lever a villager pulled to yank the links taut right in front of the *Huntress'* leading foot. Under normal circumstances, a Cataphract would be able to simply step over such an obstacle, but between the added momentum of the charge and the steep incline of the hill, the *Huntress'* foot caught. The Cataphract fell forward, crashing into the ground hard enough that Victor could feel it in his boots, even up on the hillside. Despite the trembling of his hands and the pounding of his pulse, Victor forced himself to watch. He knew he couldn't help Lady Fenvale, but he couldn't abandon her, either. That kind of fall would be jarring, true, but nothing a hardened Cataphract captain couldn't recover from. The *Huntress* was moving already, bracing one hand against the muddy, rocky ground as she ponderously started to rise.

The Behemoth surged, beaching itself at the end of the inlet, shattering the soaked wood of the dock beneath its bulk. With a groan, it opened its enormous jaws, and blue-gray smoke poured from the corners of its gaping mouth. Victor trained the spyglass on the Behemoth, expecting the creature to breathe out a stream of flame or poison, like something from the old legends. Strangely, the Behemoth lacked the pointed fangs one might expect from such a creature, even though its mouth was wide enough to devour the *Huntress* whole.

No gout of burning flame burst from the Behemoth's mouth— instead, a second, smaller Behemoth scrambled out of the open jaws. This new monster was completely different from the first. Slate gray, it had the form of a crab, all segmented legs and grasping pincers, looking to be about the same tonnage as a duelist-class Cataphract. The *Huntress* reared up on one knee to meet her opponent. She swung her sword in a hurried, awkward backhand, but the blow was still strong enough to slash clear through one of the crab-Behemoth's claws.

The *Huntress* followed through with a double-handed, cleaving blow, and her broadsword bit deep into the crab-creature's body. Its scuttling legs went limp, and a gout of smoke, not blood, streamed into the air. As the blue smoke billowed upward and mixed with that coming from the *Huntress'* own exhaust vents, Victor put the pieces together. They weren't facing Behemoths, but machines.

A Cataphract, modeled after the form of a beast instead of a man—the very concept was brilliant and blasphemous all at the same time. Once he knew what he was looking for, Victor could make out the rivets along the crab-shaped machine's hull, the ratcheting mechanisms of its leg joints, and even the exhaust chimneys poking from the rear of its compact body. A quick survey of the larger "Behemoth" showed it to be artificial as well, its "eyes" no more than portholes of smoked glass, and its shell plated with copper, hence the greenish color. Victor stared down the darkness of the whale-Cataphract's open mouth again, searching for more clues to its design and operation, but what he saw made his stomach twist in fear.

The faux-Behemoth vomited forth a second crab, then a third, then a fourth. They skittered across wet stone and broken lumber, claws snapping at the *Huntress*. Were she on level ground, Lady Fenvale could have fended them off without any trouble. But, still on one knee, with the chain tangled about her ankles, the *Huntress* was off-balance. Vulnerable.

One of the iron-plated crabs caught the *Huntress*' blade between its pincers, while another slammed into her from the opposite side. Claws clamped down on the *Huntress*' limbs, and metal groaned as the war machines grappled. The *Huntress* tried to rise, tried to get better leverage, but yet another of the machines yanked her leg out from under her, its captain clever enough and its claws nimble enough to seize the dangling anchor chain to use as a makeshift binding. The *Huntress* toppled backward, and the crabs swarmed over her, like scavengers over a corpse.

The *Huntress* bucked and fought, but it all came down to leverage. The combined strength of the crab machines was enough to pin the *Huntress* in place, helpless. Victor braced himself, waiting for one of those terrible claws to come crashing down on the *Huntress*' visor in a killing blow—but what happened instead was even worse. Several of the hooded "villagers" sprinted over, nimbly jumping up onto the *Huntress*' breastplate, running up to her closed visor. Victor watched them stuff something between the viewing slits, then heard a muffled pop. A cloud of red, acrid smoke rose from the gaps in the *Huntress*' visor, until the metal flew open. Lady Fenvale leaped out with a sword in one hand and a pistol in the other.

Half-blind, coughing, and surrounded, Lady Fenvale still fought like a woman possessed. She gunned down her nearest opponent, flung the empty pistol at the face of the next, then plunged into the ring of her enemies. She hacked away with her saber, and two more of the hooded men fell, streaming blood. Undaunted by Lady Fenvale's fury, the others closed in, pulling long, terribly familiar lengths of chain from beneath their cloaks. As Lady Fenvale lunged, a chain whipped out and tangled around her sword arm. Another chain caught her around the waist, and another one snared her ankles. The hooded assassins pulled their chains taut, binding Lady Fenvale as surely as the crab machines had captured the *Huntress*. One of them kicked the sword from Lady Fenvale's hand, and the rest of the assassins (at least those still standing) piled onto her, thoroughly binding her in loops of chain. She kicked and struggled, but the hooded men still hauled her off into one of the larger houses.

The thick wooden walls of the house muffled Lady Fenvale's shouting and curses, and a chilling silence fell over the village.

In the quiet, all Victor could hear was how fast his heart was beating.

CHAPTER 13

With speed borne of panic, the drovers unhitched the team of horses from the supply wagon, climbed onto their unsaddled backs, and galloped off. One of them might have offered to take Victor along, but he couldn't remember. Instead, Victor's boots remained glued to the muddy road, and his fingers clenched around his small brass telescope.

Below, the "villagers" of Clam-Rake didn't bother with disguises any longer. The scuttling, multi-legged Cataphracts arrayed themselves in a line, and soon the larger, whale-shaped Cataphract disgorged more and more of its crab-shaped cargo. About half of them had lighter armor and lacked the scissoring claws of their fellows. Instead, each one had a platform atop its body, on which a large-bore cannon was mounted.

Victor studied their design, impressed. The machines' additional legs offered the stability needed to fire a cannon accurately, and the broad, flat body gave the gunners someplace to stand. It wasn't without weaknesses, however; the lack of armor and melee weaponry meant that the artillery crab would be helpless if even a skirmisher were able to close in. Which was what the front line of heavier Cataphracts was for, Victor mused.

What Victor had thought were piles of supplies by the docks were, in fact, even more of the machines. Their crews yanked the concealing sailcloth away, then set about lighting their alchemical furnaces so they could clatter into formation next to their fellows. There were at least two, possibly three squadrons' worth of Cataphracts on display—enough tonnage to overwhelm Braveharbor's defenses and seize control of the North Coast. They must have been smuggling machines and men in for weeks—whoever they were.

Victor stared through his spyglass until his eye ached, searching for sigils, banners, any sort of clue of just who could marshal such a force. But the crab-shaped Cataphracts were unmarked—just plain, dull steel. With designs like that, there would be no question of who was on which side, and therefore no need for fancy banners or ornate heraldry.

The anonymous invaders kept busy, preparing their war machines to march. A few cloaked men with muskets had been posted to watch the road, but the rest of them were hard at work unloading the invasion force. At least they hadn't sent out any scouts yet, and so Victor remained safe. Or at least as safe as someone trapped in the path of a strange enemy army could be.

Lily picked up on Victor's anxiety and gave a faint whine of her own. Victor supposed it was for the best that the dog couldn't understand just what had happened. If she knew Lady Fenvale had been captured, the fearsome mastiff would have bolted straight into the village to rescue her—and likely got herself killed in the process. Thankfully, she stayed close to Victor, to the point where she often leaned her muscled bulk against him, as if to ensure he wasn't going anywhere. On the one hand, Lily's literal dogged loyalty at least provided Victor with some degree of safety. On the other, it also meant that he couldn't scribble a letter of warning and tie it to the big dog's collar, sending her off to find help. Not that Victor expected much help was available. The closest Cataphracts were still at Braveharbor, several days away. And even then, Prince Edval didn't have a large enough force to do more than slow the invaders, provided he left his city walls to begin with.

Which meant he was on his own.

Victor got to work.

The first thing he did was arm himself; as Victor had expected, Lady Fenvale had a small arsenal packed away in her luggage. Victor hung a rapier and matching dagger from his belt, then loaded a pair of flintlock pistols, hoping the whole while he wouldn't need them. Victor planned to foist the weaponry on Lady Fenvale, provided she was still in any condition to use them. She had to be,

Victor told himself. The invaders had taken her alive when they could have easily killed her instead. There had to be a reason for it.

Would they try to hold her for ransom? And if they did, who would even pay? Or would the invaders torture her for information? Or, well, they could try to. Lady Fenvale was invincible. She wouldn't break. Though every minute Victor waited was another minute for the countess' captors to apply the knives, or hot irons, or whatever other sadistic tools they might have at their disposal.

Victor shook his head, dispelling the thought. Tallying his resources proved a far more productive use of his brainpower, as well as a distracting one. He slung a tool bag across his chest and loaded it with gear he might need. He took care to wrap individual tools with scraps of cloth, so they wouldn't clink against each other as he moved. Once he figured out what he would carry with him, Victor went through the rest of the wagon. As he picked out particularly useful pieces of equipment, he started to concoct a plan. His hands moved under their own accord, fitting parts and pieces together into new, improvised configurations. Once he was done, he dug a cloak out of Lady Fenvale's baggage and rolled it in the mud until it looked vaguely similar to the ragged attire of the invaders below. He didn't expect the disguise to hold up under close scrutiny, but it might do at a distance. If nothing else, the cloak concealed the weapons Victor had stuffed into his belt. By the time he finished his hurried preparations, the sun had just begun to sink below the western horizon, and a steady drizzle soaked everything in sight.

Wrapped in his muddy cloak, Lily close at his side, Victor headed for the occupied village. He veered off from the main row, taking cover in the lengthening shadow of the hill. No guards shouted or shot at him, and Victor didn't fall on his ass, so he supposed he did a good job of it. As they got closer and closer to Clam-Rake, Lily lowered herself into a hunter's crouch, proving surprisingly stealthy for such a large animal.

More than his disguise, more than the evening shadows, what kept Victor unseen was the fact that most of the invaders had better things to do. There were guards, but only a handful, watching the road instead of the rocky ground on either side of it. The rest of the unknown invaders went back and forth in little clusters, hauling supplies and ammunition to the arrayed Cataphracts. They tied bundles and crates onto the backs of each of the crab machines, like saddlebags on a pack mule. The cargo alone was telling; no Cataphract captain would allow their machine to be used as a beast of burden, not even Lady Fenvale.

Thought of the countess made Victor move faster.

He skirted the edge of the village and flattened his back against a thatch-roofed storehouse to stay out of sight. Victor's heart hammered harder and harder, every second he went undiscovered only making him more anxious. He leaned against the wooden wall, sparing a precious moment to catch his breath. It was only when he stopped moving that Victor noticed the faint, flickering light coming from gaps between the boards and heard the voices of someone speaking inside.

"We should kill her."

There was no doubt as to whom they were talking about—Victor didn't know whether to celebrate Lady Fenvale's survival or to worry twice as hard. He at least had the peace of mind to stay still and listen harder, turning his head to press an ear against the thin wooden wall.

"The strictures are clear, Commander." The second man had an odd echo to his voice, as if he were speaking into a hollow metal box. "She must be allowed the opportunity to fix her link to ours."

"She'll never join us, you know that," said the first voice.

"Perhaps you are correct. But she may yet surprise us. Just think of what the woman would be capable of, were she to be enlightened."

"I already know what she's capable of. She killed five of my men, and that was after they hit her with scorch-smoke. She's dangerous."

"Which means she can be useful," the metallic voice replied, calm. "Just think of what valuable information she could give us, information that even our spies cannot provide. Or better yet, if her fury could be turned against a worthier target—"

"We don't have the time to break her," the first voice said. "We don't even have time to talk to her. We've been discovered, and the longer we wait, the more time our enemies will have to prepare. It's only a matter of time before someone notices the missing Cataphract and comes looking for it. For all we know, that woman could have a whole squadron marching to rescue her right now."

Slowly, silently, Victor crouched down to peer through the gap in the storehouse's wall. Inside, various sacks and barrels had been pushed aside, clearing room for an old table, piled with maps and papers, lit by a wrought-silver oil lantern. The two men standing around the table were richly dressed, in stark contrast to their humble surroundings. The first man wore a stiff black tunic, undecorated but obviously a uniform of some sort. Old enough that his brown hair was streaked with silver, the man had the severe look of one used to killing. He had the tools for it, too: a brace of pistols hung from holsters across his chest, and a straight-bladed sword rested at his left hip.

The second man, the one with the metallic voice, was shorter, balder, and far stranger. Several gold necklaces lay draped around his neck, and a fist-sized metal box rested just above his sternum. At first, Victor thought it was just part of the bald man's jewelry, but closer examination revealed that the metal had been embedded into his flesh via alchemic surgery. Victor caught his tongue between his teeth before he could swear or cry out in recognition. There was only one nation that would alter its leaders so. Another studied look at the pair confirmed Victor's suspicions as he spotted the thin silver chain hanging between the sleeve of the bald man's robe and a loop at the back of the commander's belt. There was only one reason for the pair to be connected like that.

They were Brethren of the Chain.

Once Victor saw it, the pieces all clicked into place. The Behemoth ship allowed the Brethren to move an invasion force in unnoticed; it could travel underwater for at least short distances. Even when it had been spotted, it was at a distance, and its bestial disguise allowed its true nature to remain unknown. With the number of men they'd brought with them, it would be a trivial matter to capture a tiny fishing hamlet to use as a staging ground for the rest of the invasion.

Victor wondered what had happened to Clam-Rake's original inhabitants. Had they been captured and shackled as part of the Brethren's perverse doctrine? Shipped back to to their home port? Or had the villagers been merely slaughtered and their bodies dumped into the ocean? Victor wasn't sure if he wanted to know.

Inside, the Brethren kept talking.

"You make a compelling point, Commander," said the bald man. "We shall speak with the prisoner. So long as you promise not to shoot her."

"Only if she makes me."

The bald man sighed. "I suppose that will have to do. Now come." He looped the thin chain around his palm and tugged the commander along, like someone taking a dog for a walk. Stunningly, the hard-faced officer followed without complaining about the humiliation: more evidence of the Brethren's bizarre philosophy. Their chains clinked softly as they walked out of the storehouse and out of sight. Victor stood up and blinked a few times, letting his eyes adjust back to the dimming twilight after peering into the better-lit storeroom. He risked a peek around the corner, tracking the progress of the commander and the robed man. The other Brethren cleared a path in front of the two men, crossing their wrists in front of their chests in salute.

The formality of the salutes at least offered Victor some valuable opportunities. For one, the metal-voiced man and the officer chained to him were of enough importance that the other Brethren made it a point to work faster and harder as they passed, which distracted them enough for Victor to creep from the cover of one building to the next. Moreover, Victor soon deduced where they were keeping Lady Fenvale. A pair of spear-wielding guards stood posted in front of one of the driftwood shacks. Their chains rattled as they saluted.

Victor took a longer, roundabout route to the same house, circling the edge of the village, staying out of sight. Miraculously, Lady Fenvale's erstwhile prison didn't have any guards posted around back. The Brethren must have been more concerned with Lady Fenvale getting out than anyone getting in. By the time Victor got there, the two Brethren officials had already started their interrogation. Victor put his ear to the thin boards and listened.

"That may be the stupidest thing anyone has ever said to me." Lady Fenvale laughed, bitter and mirthless. "They must have scooped your brains out when they put your voice box in, Speaker."

At the sound of her mistress' voice, Lily's floppy ears perked forward. Victor winced and shushed the big dog; the last thing they needed was for Lily to smash through the door and bring every last Brethren in the village down on them. Lily must have understood, somehow, as she stayed still and stealthy, only giving a soft, plaintive whine. Inside, the Brethren continued their interrogation.

"Watch your tongue, or I'll cut it out," the commander said.

"Stop posturing, the both of you," said the man with the metallic voice.

Victor found a gap in the boards and peered inside. Lady Fenvale sat with her back to Victor, shackled to a sturdy chair in an otherwise empty room. Lengths of gray steel chain wrapped around her like a metal cocoon, trailing off to a rusted but still solid anchor. The bald man—the Speaker, Victor corrected himself—stood in front of her with his hands held in front of his belly, tucked into the sleeves of his robe. The commander, meanwhile, stood near the room's only door, as far from Lady Fenvale as the chain around his waist allowed. He held a lantern in one hand and kept the other close to his pistol.

"And I'm not helping you," Lady Fenvale said.

"Think of the lives you could save." Despite the faint metallic echo of the Speaker's artificial voice, his words still carried genuine emotion behind them. "With your assistance, we could take Braveharbor with a minimum of bloodshed—"

"Those people would be better off dead than under your yoke," Lady Fenvale spat back.

"And who are you to make that decision?" The Speaker tut-tutted like a scolding schoolteacher. "Just because you know how to operate a war machine doesn't make you any wiser, any better than the next man. And here I had hoped you wouldn't be as arrogant and foolish as the rest of your countrymen."

"You've come to enslave us, and I'm the arrogant one?"

"Slavery? What a puerile understanding of our philosophy." The Speaker sighed. "It can take years to truly appreciate the beauty of our doctrine. But let me put things in terms even you will understand. We have come to bring enlightenment, connection—civilization. Among the Brethren, everyone is provided for. Everyone has a place in the Great Chain." The Speaker took his hands out of his sleeve and let links of silver chain dribble through his fingers, reverently. "Even you, Countess. You have a rare opportunity to choose what your place will be."

"To choose between gold chain and iron, you mean," Lady Fenvale said. "All you're attempting is to replace one hierarchy with another."

"There must be an order to things, yes," the Speaker said. "I have been fortunate enough, worthy enough to hold the title of Speaker. But it is an honor that I earned—unlike your own title, 'Countess.'" He made the title an epithet. "We do not hold to antiquated ideas of 'noble blood' or any similar nonsense. Leovaix is an archaic, inefficient relic, governed by an impenetrable morass of unjust laws and unfathomable traditions. Someday, it will collapse. All it will take is a bad harvest or a succession crisis or some greedy duke deciding he doesn't want to pay taxes, and then it will be war. Famine. Chaos. It's only a matter of time. The people of Leovaix, like all people in the world, need the Brethren of the Chain to bind them together."

"You've got that part right." Lady Fenvale shook her head. "As soon as word gets out, the whole of Leovaix will unite long enough to crush you, just like my father did."

"Ah. Your machine was at Osterbridge, wasn't it? How ironic." The Speaker let his chain fall slack and tucked his hands back into his sleeves again. "Our defeat there was a turning point. It taught us that the old ways, your ways, were holding us back. We developed new tactics and forged new weapons that your antiquated strategy cannot comprehend. This country shall fall, Countess, and the world will be better for it."

"Give it up, Speaker," the officer on the other end of the chain grumbled. "I told you she wouldn't listen."

"Indeed you did, Commander. But our prisoner may yet prove useful. She is to remain unharmed until then, understood?"

"Understood, Speaker. I'll double the guard—"

"No need." The bald man waved a hand airily. "The men would be put to better use elsewhere, especially if we're to remain on schedule."

"But Speaker, this woman—"

"Is not our primary objective. Carry out your orders."

"As you wish, Speaker." The commander thumped his chest in salute.

The Speaker looked down at Lady Fenvale, a pitying expression on his face. "I can only hope you will change your mind once you see the good we're doing. Good night, Countess." And with that, the Speaker and his attached officer walked out of the room, and the guards closed the wooden door behind them, leaving Lady Fenvale steel-bound in the dark. Victor waited for a few minutes, in case the guards came in to check on her, then got to work once it was clear they wouldn't. He slid a long, wide-bladed dagger out of its scabbard and used it as a makeshift pry bar, working at the loosest board in the wall. So long as Lady Fenvale kept her guards distracted, they wouldn't hear Victor working at the wall—or so he hoped. Splinters dug into Victor's fingers as he pulled the board away, but his heart pounded too fast for the pain to register. The board popped free, opening up a gap about as wide as Victor's forearm. He carefully laid the board on the ground—

—and Lily forced her way through.

The gap was barely wider than the big dog's head, but she didn't let that stop her. Once her shoulders butted up against the wall, she braced her feet and pushed, hard enough to make the boards on either side of her head bow and then snap. She wriggled her way into the shack and immediately bounded over to Lady Fenvale. She planted her front paws on the countess' lap and insistently leaned up to lick and slobber at her face.

Lady Fenvale laughed—the sound was genuine, soft. "Easy, girl."

Victor ducked through the now-larger hole, and Lady Fenvale twisted around as far as the chains allowed to face him. Her eyes were teary and red, but she smiled nonetheless. "About time you got here," she said.

"You knew we were coming? How?" Victor kept his voice low, so the guards outside wouldn't hear them.

"Lily has a very distinctive smell. Especially when she's wet," Lady Fenvale said. "But how did you make it past the guards?"

"I had a little practice sneaking in past curfew at university."

"And they say higher education isn't practical," Lady Fenvale said, and pulled at her chains again. "Did they teach lockpicking there, too?'

"After a fashion." Victor hurried over and crouched down to examine Lady Fenvale's shackles. He hefted a thick padlock in his palm, then reached into his bag of tools. "A lock is a rather simple mechanism when compared to the inner workings of a Cataphract. Once I understand its underlying principles—" He slid a thin metal shim into the keyhole and probed around, envisioning the workings within. Once Victor felt the push of a spring within the lock, he applied pressure at just the right angle, and the bolt popped open. Victor repeated the process on the other locks holding Lady Fenvale in place, and she wriggled free of her chains like a snake shedding an iron skin.

"If you ever give up on engineering, you could make a living as a burglar." Lady Fenvale stretched her limbs and gave Lily a pet between the ears.

"That might be a safer occupation." Victor undid the sword belt around his waist and handed it over to Lady Fenvale, who buckled it on without being asked.

"And where's the fun in that?" Lady Fenvale took a brace of pistols from Victor as well. "They haven't moved the *Huntress*, have they?"

Victor shook his head.

"Good." Pistol in hand, Lady Fenvale ducked through the hole in the wall. "Once I get her on her feet again—"

"The Brethren's Cataphracts will just drag you back down before you can get her furnace fully stoked," Victor whispered as he followed suit.

"I won't abandon—"

Victor held up a hand, and Lady Fenvale, to his mild surprise, went quiet. "I'm not asking you to. Which is why I'm going to provide a distraction."

"I'm not abandoning you either, Victor. Especially not after this."

"I'm certainly not asking you to do that." Victor took off his glasses and rubbed at his face. "I'll meet you at the *Huntress*. Just wait until my signal to get her moving. If I make enough of a commotion, the Brethren won't think to stop you until it's too late."

"Better than nothing," Lady Fenvale said. "So what will the signal be?"

Victor leaned around the corner of the shack and watched the Brethren rush about, hauling supplies out of the whale-ship to load onto the four-legged Cataphracts in the village. A plan coalesced in his brain, dangerous enough to make his mouth go dry and his stomach turn. Still, he put on a brave smile and nodded to Lady Fenvale. "You'll know it when you see it."

CHAPTER 14

One look up at the night sky told Victor how well the Brethren had planned their invasion. Moving under the full moon allowed them to work through the night without wasting candles or lantern oil, and the higher tides caused by the full moon would in turn make it easier to sail their submersible Cataphract ship into the bay. Just by watching the Brethren work, Victor could see the complexity of their strategy: an enormous machine with chained men in place of springs and cogs.

Victor knew the more complicated a machine was, the more places it could break.

Lily refused to leave Lady Fenvale's side, so Victor was left to creep through the village on his own. It proved easier than he'd expected. The Brethren were so focused on their given tasks—and only on those tasks—that Victor could creep from the shadow of one building to the next without being seen. He circled around the village until he got to the shoreline.. He took off his glasses, put them in a small case, then stowed that case in his pocket. Thusly prepared, he eased himself into the ink-dark sea. As the chilly water seeped into his boots and clothing, Victor clamped his teeth together and tried not to think of what the seawater would do to his tools. Which, in its way, he found somewhat reassuring, as it at least kept him from dwelling on the horrible tortures the Brethren would subject him to if he were caught. The sting of salt water on his scraped knuckles paled in comparison to the creatively sadistic devices Victor's imagination could come up with.

Crouched low in the water, boots sinking into the muck, Victor waded towards the metal sea-Behemoth beached on the shore. As he got closer, he could only marvel at the scale of the machine. The copper-plated craft was even larger than a siegebreaker—though Victor imagined most of its volume was empty, devoted to cargo. Blue alchemical smoke wafted up from exhaust vents along the Behemoth's spine, no doubt modeled after the water spouting of whales or dolphins. Part of Victor wished he could study the machine's design under better circumstances, though he knew it was extremely unlikely that any of the Brethren would share the schematics with the enemy.

He'd just have to get a look himself.

The Brethren crews worked steadily, efficiently—and predictably. Victor waited for an opening, the brief pause between one crew of Brethren hauling something out of the whale-machine and the next gang marching into its open gullet. The metal of the machine's gangplank-jaw was cold and slippery beneath Victor's fingers as he pulled himself out of the water, and his boots squelched wetly with each step. He stumbled into the machine as quickly as he dared and took refuge behind a stack of barrels.

Like the outside, the interior of the whale-machine mimicked the anatomy of a great beast: arched steel struts for ribs, thick brass pipes for veins, taut steel cabling for tendons. And somewhere, deep within, would be its heart: an alchemical furnace. Victor could already feel the furnace's residual heat, and as he went deeper into the machine, the air grew thicker with steam. Past the cargo hold in the "belly" of the whale-machine, the mechanisms grew more complex, packed in so close that Victor often had to turn sideways to wriggle through. He passed ballast tanks, pressure valves, motive gears, and more intricate devices that he couldn't identify at a glance. Yet, even in the dim light, surrounded by unfamiliar machinery, Victor identified the basic principles behind the whale-machine's operation. The motive gears were simpler than those of a proper Cataphract. Larger, too. The whale-machine wasn't built to fight; it was only meant to swim and carry its underwater cargo from one place to another. The enormous fins at the end of the tail provided forward motion by moving up and down, while smaller rudders mounted along the hull steered it. The helm would be at the "head" of the enormous machine, with control cabling strung up along the top of the cargo bay. Once Victor had identified how the whale-machine worked (at least in theory), it didn't take him long to follow the mass of ever-complicating pipes and cables until he found what he was looking for.

In a proper Cataphract, the alchemical furnace was housed deep within the torso, surrounded by steel plating so it couldn't be ruptured by an errant sword thrust. Whoever had designed the whale-machine had at least followed a similar principle, locking the invaluable heart of the machine away in a steel vault, latches sealed with intricate locks far beyond Victor's modest lockpicking skill. But Victor knew he didn't have to get at the furnace directly. Instead, he examined the pipes that led in and out of the vault, and quickly identified their purpose.

Victor wiped his palms clean of sweat and seawater (or at least tried to) and fished tools out of his bag. First, he located the spools and pulleys of the control cables, the link from the whale-machine's helm to its driving engine. In the first true design flaw he saw since climbing inside the machine, Victor noted the control cables were of plain, braided rope, not twined steel cabling. It must have been a weight-saving measure, or possibly a budgetary one. No matter what it was, Victor seized on the opportunity and used his dagger to saw through the taut ropes, until they were only held in place by a few strands. As soon as someone at the helm pulled on a control lever and put pressure on them, they'd snap.

Victor went to the valves next. He fitted an adjustable wrench around the furnace's air intake valve and opened it as far as it would go, then did the opposite to the exhaust stack and the pipes branching off to the motive gears. He braced his feet and pulled hard on the output valves, sealing them so tight that the valve handle broke off.

With more air going into the furnace, it would burn hotter and produce more power. With everything else sealed off, all that power would have nowhere to go. Pressure would build up steadily, until it found a catastrophic release. And with the control cables frayed just short of breaking, whoever was at the helm wouldn't be able to activate the emergency shutoff. Without a careful study of the machine's schematics, Victor couldn't know which pipe or component would break first, but he knew he didn't want to be around when it happened.

Sabotage complete, Victor put his tools away and slunk towards the cargo bay. The sounds of heavy footsteps and rattling chains echoed off the arched ceiling, announcing the arrival of the next work crew. Despite the sweltering heat of the engine room, a chill rolled up Victor's spine. He forced himself to breathe steadily, then picked up a bulky canvas-wrapped bundle and hefted it on his shoulder. The awkward weight of the supplies made Victor sway precariously back and forth, but through strength born of desperation, he kept himself from falling. Victor steeled himself, then started walking for the open mouth of the cargo bay. He tried to keep the bundle on his shoulder interposed between his face and the Brethren work crews, while also staying close enough to the groups of chained men in order to pass himself off as one of them. At a glance, at least. Hopefully, everyone else would keep too busy to notice another set of hands helping out.

With aching shoulders and a racing pulse, Victor hauled his load across the cargo bay and fell in at the end of a line of similarly laden men. Just as he stepped off the metal gangplank and onto the muddy ground, he staggered, taking a moment to adjust to the softer ground.

"Menial." The Speaker's metallic voice carried across the village. "You falter under your burden. Do you require assistance?"

Victor froze. As soon as the Brethren got a closer, better look at his unshackled wrists, they'd be all too happy to see him chained. He braced his feet, afraid to speak and give himself away through some breach of protocol and ceremony. How was a so-called Menial supposed to address someone as important as a Speaker? Or would silence be just as damning? Victor opened his mouth to say something, anything—

Which was when the ship exploded.

The open mouth of the whale-ship funneled the sound of bursting metal out across the village, loud enough to echo for miles around. Victor felt the explosion more than he heard it, and sprawled face forward onto the damp ground. Clouds of smoke, both blue and black, roiled out of the whale-ship's mouth. Another explosion followed, then a second and a third, as each broken component cascaded into another. Men shouted: in fear, in pain, in sheer confusion. A perverse pride bubbled up in Victor's chest; he was a better saboteur than he thought.

"Remain calm!" The Speaker's unnaturally loud voice boomed, even louder than the explosions. "Menials, help your fellows get clear! The supplies can be replaced—you cannot! You have greater purpose than to die here today! Rally to me, Brethren!" At the

Speaker's urging, the chained work gangs scrambled to their feet and fled from the burning whale-ship. Victor left the bundle of supplies in the mud and bolted for the *Huntress*, barely a pistol shot away.

Ponderous as a waking drunk, the *Huntress* pushed herself up to one knee. Some of the sentries snapped off musket shots, only for the balls to glance harmlessly from her armor plating. The *Huntress* turned and stooped low, holding her left hand to Victor, palm up. The Cataphract's visor levered open to reveal Lady Fenvale and Lily, squeezed into the helm-seat side by side. "Get on!" she shouted, then pulled a lever to slam the visor closed again.

Victor flung himself into the *Huntress*' hand and slammed into the unyielding metal. He wheezed for breath and tried not to think about how an accidental push of a control lever could dash him to the ground or crush him in the *Huntress*' massive fist. These fears proved to be unfounded, as the *Huntress* held her left hand level and close to her breastplate with careful deliberation. Gears turned and metal clanked as she stood, sword in one hand, trembling engineer in the other. Victor looked up at the Cataphract, feeling like a tiny child cradled by a very large, very protective parent. Blue smoke puffed rhythmically from the *Huntress*' vents; Lady Fenvale had already activated the bellows for extra power. She'd need it.

The Speaker's voice rang out, tense and shrill with barely contained fury, amazingly louder than the surrounding chaos. "You cannot win! You are outnumbered! Outmatched! These underhanded tactics offer you only a fleeting advantage! The Brethren of the Chain shall not be defeated so easily!"

In reply, Lady Fenvale turned the *Huntress* about and brought her sword down on the nearest resting crab-machine, shearing straight through one of its legs. The machine toppled to the side like a three-legged table, and the cannon mounted on its back broke loose of its mooring to tumble down into the mud. But even as the one crab-machine collapsed, more of its fellows moved in. One of them reached out with its grasping claws, but Lady Fenvale knocked them aside with a wide sweep of the *Huntress*' blade. She twisted at the waist and lowered her shoulder to ram the crab-machine. The Brethren Cataphract braced all four legs, but the *Huntress*' greater mass won out, and the crab-machine flipped over onto its back. The *Huntress* raised one massive foot and stomped on her opponent's belly, crumpling the thinner metal beneath her boot until its helplessly flailing limbs went still.

All around them, more of the Brethren's machines shuddered to life. Lady Fenvale kept moving, not letting herself get bogged down by the overwhelming numbers. The *Huntress'* sword rose and fell, hacking a path through the scuttling metal horde. Pincers dug furrows into the *Huntress'* armor, but Lady Fenvale powered through, refusing to be dragged down as she had before. Victor clung to the *Huntress'* thumb with both arms, watching the battle through the gaps in her door-sized fingers. A crab-machine lunged forward, clamping both its claws around the *Huntress'* left arm, threatening to shake Victor from his precarious perch. Before Victor could scream in shrill terror, the *Huntress'* sword hammered downward, hitting her attacker hard enough that Victor felt the reverberations through his whole body.

"Victor!" Lady Fenvale shouted. "Are you all right?"

Victor swallowed, then waved up at the *Huntress'* visor, signaling that he was still alive.

"Good! Now hold on!"

The *Huntress* yanked her sword free, pushed through a gap in her attackers, and charged up the hill leading away from the village. Within minutes, they put enough distance behind her that the Speaker's self-important ranting bled into the background. Lady Fenvale pushed the *Huntress* hard, long, pounding strides coming one after another. As they climbed the hill, Victor saw the supply wagon up ahead and remembered how he'd planned for this very moment.

He thumped a hand against the *Huntress'* breastplate. "Stop here!"

The *Huntress* didn't stop, but Lady Fenvale at least opened her visor. "What?"

"We need to stop here!"

"Are you mad? The Brethren are still after us—"

"Which is why we need to stop. I planned for this. Trust me."

140

Lady Fenvale frowned.

The *Huntress* stopped anyway and lowered Victor to the ground. He hopped out of the Cataphract's hand and looked down the hill. As Victor had predicted, a trio of crab-machines scuttled after them in close formation. Victor ran to the wagon and yanked away the oilcloth he'd draped over its contents. To his relief, he found the oilcloth had done its job, and that most everything was dry.

Dry enough to burn.

Between two kegs of gear grease, a large jug of lamp oil, and a flask of Lady Fenvale's gunpowder, Victor had more than enough to improvise an incendiary. Even the oilcloth cover itself would burn. Victor lit the oil-soaked rags he'd thrust into the barrel of grease, then hopped backwards as flames flared up, even faster than he'd anticipated. He shielded his face from the heat, then yanked at the ropes tied through the wooden blocks holding the wagon's wheels in place. Without brakes or blocks to stop it, gravity took over, and the wagon rolled downhill towards the Brethren's war machines, a hundred yards or so behind. The flaming wagon built up speed and momentum as it hurtled downhill. It passed beneath the lead crab-machine and smashed into one of its rear legs, shattering in a spray of burning oil and timber. The crab-machine staggered sideways and plowed into its fellows.

"Impressive." Lady Fenvale looked over the chaos. "But it won't stop them."

"But it'll at least slow them down." Victor hopped back onto the *Huntress*' open hand. "Which is why we'd better get moving."

CHAPTER 15

Stride by stride, the *Huntress* fled from Clam-Rake, moving far faster on the retreat than their earlier arrival. Even when it became clear they weren't being pursued, Lady Fenvale kept the *Huntress* moving at a steady, constant pace. She marched straight through the night, not slowed by an escort or supply wagon.

Victor spent the first leg of the journey cradled in the *Huntress'* palm, an exhausting ordeal in its own right. The helm-seat of a Cataphract was surrounded by cushions and mounted on springs meant to protect the captain from the inevitable jolts and jostling one would expect from three stories' worth of metal plating and moving parts. The *Huntress'* left hand had no such comforts, and so Victor found himself bruised in new and unexpected ways.

They stopped at dawn, only long enough for Lady Fenvale to wake up the owner of a roadside inn. She still had her Writ of Acquisition and made good use of it in securing provisions, as well as a horse for Victor. This done, she warned the innkeeper of the impending invasion and took to the *Huntress'* helm-seat once more, this time with Victor and Lily trotting along behind her. They pressed on straight through the next day, to the point where even Lily's canine enthusiasm began to flag. Victor tried sleeping in the saddle, but it was a fitful process, as every time he began to drift off, he'd jerk himself back awake in fear of falling from his mount. Bleary-eyed, Victor breathed a sigh of relief as the walls of Braveharbor came into view, their gray stone painted red by the setting sun. The mere sight of the high walls and the Cataphracts guarding them was enough to make Victor forget about his omnipresent aches.

The main gate stood open, with the *Challenge* posted outside, watching the main road. Upon sighting the *Huntress*, the *Challenge* raised her axe in salute, and Lady Fenvale mirrored the gesture, hoisting the *Huntress'* battle-chipped broadsword in reply. She lowered the blade, resting it on the *Huntress'* shoulder as she brought her duelist to a halt in front of the barred gate. The *Challenge* raised her visor, and her captain, Baron Halborn, leaned forward. He was a middle-aged man with an impressive yellow mustache, the drooping tips long enough to sway back and forth whenever he spoke.

"Ho there, Countess! Back so soon? Your riders just arrived yesterday. The Behemoth wasn't too much for you, was it?" Baron Halborn chortled. "Looks like the beast gave you a proper thrashing! I presume the Behemoth's in even worse shape?"

"It's not a Behemoth," Lady Fenvale snapped back, her speaking cone only amplifying the barely concealed anger in her voice. "It's a damned invasion. And it'll be too much for all of us if we're not ready. Now let me through; I must speak with Prince Edval."

Baron Halborn's cheery smile faded, and he quickly moved the *Challenge* out of the way to let the *Huntress* through. Lady Fenvale didn't march directly for the palace. Instead, she headed for the Bell and Kettle. She eased the *Huntress* into a crouch in the small stable yard behind the inn, then climbed down from the helm. Her sudden, unexpected arrival drew a small crowd of nosy onlookers, along with Lieutenant Iral and a handful of his dragoons.

"How are you holding up, Victor?" Lady Fenvale walked over to a barrel of rainwater and splashed some over her face. She had bags under her eyes, her dark hair barely held back in a ponytail, and her clothes were caked with dust and dried blood. Even still, the countess carried herself proudly, bearing the signs of exhaustion like battle scars.

"Do you want an honest answer?" He eased himself from the saddle, feeling less like he'd been riding a horse and more like he'd been trampled by one. Lily, meanwhile, plopped down in the *Huntress'* shadow with a tired grunt.

"At least you've still got a sense of humor. Good." Lady Fenvale pulled a white linen handkerchief out of her tunic jacket and dried her face. "Go inside, eat something, and get a few hours' rest. After that, I want you to go over the *Huntress*. We're going to need her at peak performance for what comes next."

Victor nodded and looked up at the kneeling Cataphract, her armor battle-damaged and road-filthy. But the wounds weren't deep; the *Huntress'* inner workings were still intact, and her furnace still burned strong. She could still fight, even if she'd be an embarrassment in a parade. "I can start now, actually."

Lady Fenvale shook her head. "Food and sleep first, Victor. The last thing I need is you leaving a wrench somewhere it doesn't belong because you're too tired to know better."

"I promise you, that won't be a—"

"Food. Sleep. That is an order, Chief Engineer Brinden." She patted him on the shoulder, then looked past him, towards the handful of their dragoons, who waited near the back door of the inn. "Lieutenant Iral, I'm leaving the Chief Engineer under your supervision. Make sure he does not touch the *Huntress* until he can at least stand up straight."

"Of course, Countess." Lieutenant Iral bowed. "How else can we be of assistance?"

"Get me a fresh horse—I need to get to Prince Edval's palace as soon as possible." She paused, then looked down at her rumpled, stained attire. "And a clean shirt wouldn't hurt, either."

Per Lady Fenvale's orders, Victor scarfed down the better part of a roast chicken, drank a tall flagon of dark beer, and passed out on a straw mattress without bothering to take off his boots. His sleep was fitful and dreamless, but by the time he woke the next morning, he felt close to human once more. He rolled out of bed (nearly tripping over Lily's dozing bulk in the process), picked up his bag of tools, and went out to check on the *Huntress*. The duelist still knelt where Lady Fenvale had left her in the stable yard, which Victor took as a good sign. Things weren't bad enough that the *Huntress* needed to charge off to battle.

Yet.

After days of riding, sneaking, and running from one place to another, the basic tasks of maintenance were soothingly familiar. The weight of a wrench in Victor's hand reassured him—doubly so with the knowledge that he was putting the tool to its proper use, and not using it to bash someone over the back of the head. Tightening bolts, splicing cable, setting levers—each task was something that Victor knew how to do, something he had control over.

Sometime before noon, Lady Fenvale rode back from the palace. With fresh clothes and combed hair, the countess looked far better than she had the evening before, though that was a low bar to set. Victor wondered if she'd slept at the palace, or if she'd even slept at all. The countess dismounted her horse, handed her reins off to one of the waiting dragoons, and went straight to the *Huntress*. Lily galloped over and fell into step beside her mistress, tail wagging.

Lady Fenvale looked up at her Cataphract, thoughtful. "Can she fight?"

"Can she? Yes. Should she?" Victor made a wobbly gesture with his left hand. "That's debatable. I've done what I can. The *Huntress*' cables are taut, her bolts are secure, and her motive gears are greased—"

"But?" Lady Fenvale crossed her arms over her chest.

Victor winced. "There are dents in both her gauntlets, torn metal on her left greave plating, and a weak spot on the right side of her breastplate. All it would take is one lucky hit to cripple her."

"Can you fix it?" Lady Fenvale kept her voice even and her eyes on the *Huntress*, as if she could glare the dents out of her armor.

"Dents can be pounded out, and armor plating can be replaced, but—"

"I still have a Writ of Acquisition. I can get you what you need."

"There's no doubt of that, Countess Fenvale—but in addition to parts and supplies, I need time. It'll take at least a day to cut and shape patches for the outer armor, and even that's a temporary fix."

"Do what you can." Lady Fenvale rubbed at the bridge of her nose. "You may have more time than you think."

"How do you mean?

"According to Prince Edval, my … failure at Clam-Rake means I'm unfit to fight." Her shoulders stiffened, and she tapped a frustrated finger on the hilt of her saber.

"Failure?" Victor blinked. "You single-handedly fought off an entire army of Brethren so you could warn the city. How is that a failure?"

"According to His Highness, I was sent to slay a Behemoth, and have come back empty-handed. Ergo, failure."

"That's idiocy," Victor said.

"That's politics," Lady Fenvale seethed, and spat on the muddy ground.

Victor frowned. "Politics or no, the *Huntress* is one of four Cataphracts along the whole North Coast. It doesn't take a master strategist to see excluding her—er, which is to say, you—is a terrible idea."

"Prince Edval says he doesn't need the *Huntress*' help. He's going to fight the Brethren. Personally."

"Personally?" The word worked its way through Victor's brain. "You mean Prince Edval is—" He didn't finish his sentence as a long shadow passed over the stable yard.

The ground shook.

The people of Braveharbor cheered.

The *Tender Mercy of Queen Jeriel* marched for the city gates.

146

CHAPTER 16

"We shouldn't be here." Victor clapped a hand over his floppy cap as a gust of cool wind blew over the battlement and threatened to pluck it off his head.

"Perhaps." Lady Fenvale propped a boot up on the edge of the city wall and leaned forward, squinting into a spyglass. "But we're stuck in Braveharbor until the Brethren are dealt with."

"I meant here. On the wall. I should be working on the *Huntress*. And you might want to be close by, in case—" Victor chewed at the inside of his cheek and looked out at the approaching Brethren squadron. Even without a telescope, Victor could make out the alien, scuttling gait of their crab-shaped Cataphracts. "—in case things go wrong."

"The *Huntress* is close enough, and you've already done everything you can." Lady Fenvale stepped away from the wall and tugged the brim of her own hat back down to shade her eyes. "Besides, you're smarter than I am, Victor. You may see something that I don't." She handed him the small brass telescope. "And that might be what saves us."

"If you insist." Victor took the spyglass. "Though honestly, you're probably more qualified when it comes to gauging combat prowess and tactics and the like."

"Just watch," Lady Fenvale said.

The *Tender Mercy of Queen Jeriel* was huge, even for a siegebreaker. Her broad shoulders, thick limbs, and enormous war hammer all held promises of power and destruction. She could fight whole squadrons, whole armies of the enemy; the baroque scrollwork on her armor listed the battles in which she had done so, and the honors she'd been awarded afterward. Even her name was imposing, given the amount of gruesome legends surrounding the ancient ruler for whom the *Queen Jeriel* had been named.

Prince Edval sat at his Cataphract's helm-seat, dressed in ornate, polished armor to match that of his machine. He left *Queen Jeriel*'s visor open so he could be seen. While the royal family owned several Cataphracts with ancient and honorable service records, it was a rare thing to see someone in the direct line of succession captain them personally instead of giving the honor to a trusted vassal. As such, Braveharbor's best and brightest had crowded along the wall to see Prince Edval go to war. Retainers, officials, and other well-dressed hangers-on waved their fans and handkerchiefs up at the prince, trying to catch his attention, while liveried servants brought them warm drinks and sweet snacks. The whole affair reminded Victor of how he'd watched the battle of Osterbridge, years before. He hoped the upcoming battle would end as well as that one had.

Lady Fenvale had picked a spot on the wall unfashionably far from the *Tender Mercy of Queen Jeriel*, that still offered clear sight lines to the surrounding countryside and the approaching army marching over it. Hundreds of yards away, the Brethren's scuttling crab-machines fanned out, forming a semicircle facing Braveharbor's main gate. Victor peered through the telescope and made a quick tally of their numbers.

"Looks like you crippled at least a few of their Cataphracts," Victor mused aloud. "There's fewer here than there were at Clam-Rake."

"Possibly,"said Lady Fenvale. "But fewer machines here could also mean they've sent some out as scouts, or to raid the countryside. They'd have to. The Brethren didn't bring any horses with them. No cavalry."

"No infantry, either." Victor swept the lens of the spyglass over the enemy line. The Brethren had a mixed formation, with the cannon-equipped Cataphracts standing between the clawed ones. "They must be using every man they've got to man the guns on the smaller machines. I don't know how they expect to hold Braveharbor. Or any other territory, for that matter."

"Unless they've just come to slaughter us all," Lady Fenvale said, grim.

"Or that." Victor lowered the spyglass before his hands could start shaking.

"We must be missing something." Lady Fenvale tapped an impatient finger on her saber's pommel. "The Brethren must have planned for this."

Victor wracked his brain, trying to think of some tiny detail he might have seen or overheard that might allow him to guess at the Brethren's strategy. Before any thoughts could coalesce in Victor's mind, Prince Edval's speaking cone–amplified voice rolled out over the city wall.

"Look at them!" Prince Edval addressed his audience of retainers and servants with haughty, casual ease. "These are the machines the Brethren have brought to face me? They crawl over the ground like so many insects! And yet, the so-called Beasthunter-Errant fled from them like a whipped cur! It is enough to make one wonder what Countess Fenvale did for my brother to give her such a useless title."

Sycophantic laughter rippled down the city wall. Lady Fenvale narrowed her eyes and flexed her grip around the hilt of her sword. Her expression grew dark enough that Victor wondered if she were a bigger danger to Prince Edval than the Brethren. A few nearby revelers noticed the countess' bristling and prudently went quiet.

"No matter!" Prince Edval went on, either unaware or unconcerned with Lady Fenvale's reaction. "Where my brother's cringing flunky has failed, I, your prince, shall prevail! Watch, my loyal subjects, and marvel as I crush these fools like the writhing vermin they are! For today, the Brethren shall feel the *Tender Mercy of Queen Jeriel*!"

Blue smoke chugged from the *Queen Jeriel*'s vents, and Prince Edval went to war. Step by ponderous step, the siegebreaker advanced on her foes. The rumbling of the *Queen Jeriel*'s stride was loud, but not loud enough to drown out the cheering and applause from the onlookers along the city wall. A salvo of firework rockets whizzed up into the air, announcing the *Queen Jeriel*'s slow advance.

Victor and Lady Fenvale watched.

"They flee!" a foppishly dressed man shouted as he watched the battle play out through a set of opera glasses. "Prince Edval has saved us all!"

Sure enough, as the *Queen Jeriel* advanced, the crab-machines clattered backwards, staying well out of the siegebreaker's reach. Braveharbor's residents celebrated the latest development, alternating between loud praises of Prince Edval's valor and creatively obscene insults about the Brethren's cowardice, hygiene, and parentage (if not in that order).

"Idiots." Seething, Lady Fenvale took the spyglass back from Victor and stared out over the battlefield. "The prince hasn't even closed the distance yet, and they're acting like he's already—oh."

"Oh?" A familiar, anxious knot tightened in Victor's stomach.

"They're baiting him. Look." She lowered the glass and pointed. As Prince Edval pushed back the center of the Brethren's line, the flanks of the semicircle closed in behind the *Queen Jeriel*. "That ass can't even see what's happening. If he's not careful, the Brethren will—"

A cannon fired.

The iron cannonball slammed into the side of the siegebreaker's breastplate, bashing a deep dent before bouncing off. The rest of the cannoneers followed suit, bombarding the *Queen Jeriel* from all directions. Cannonballs hit the steel plating over and over, like the world's largest, angriest blacksmith pounding away at his anvil. The *Queen Jeriel* endured the barrage admirably, her armor plating thick enough to turn the heavy round shot.

Or at least the first volley.

As soon as flame belched from the mouths of the cannons mounted on the back of the Brethren's Cataphracts, their crews scrambled to reload their weapons, ramming loads of powder and cannonballs down the muzzles. Chains held the crews in place atop the

Cataphracts—though Victor wasn't sure if this was a safety precaution, a punishment, or some show of their devotion. If not a combination of all three.

The Brethren kept their Cataphracts moving, keeping them just out of reach of the *Queen Jeriel*'s deadly war hammer. Undaunted, Prince Edval kept pushing forward, away from Braveharbor's walls. The *Queen Jeriel* occasionally swiped at one of the crab-machines scuttling around her. A single blow from her massive hammer would have smashed any of them to pieces, but the *Queen Jeriel* was too slow and clumsy to connect. Watching the battle, Victor was reminded of when some of his fellow students had dragged him to a bearbaiting. The bear had one leg chained to a thick post, rendering it unable to effectively fight back against the pack of snarling dogs surrounding it. The Brethren were using a similar tactic, only this time, it was like the fighting dogs had armed themselves with pistols.

"They're going to kill him." A cold mass of anxiety grew within Victor's stomach. "We've got to do something—"

"There's nothing we can do." Lady Fenvale shook her head, coming to the same grim conclusion. "Prince Edval's too far from the gates. By the time we got the *Huntress* close enough—"

The Brethren fired another salvo.

By luck or by skill, the second wave of cannon fire was better aimed than the first. One cannonball slammed into the back of the *Queen Jeriel*'s right knee, smashing through the comparatively thinner armor around the joint. Another bounced off the corner of the siegebreaker's visor, coming dangerously close to bursting through the metal and killing Prince Edval at the controls. Between her damaged knee and a shaken man at the helm, the *Queen Jeriel* listed to the side, off-balance. The Brethren seized on the opportunity, and the clawed Cataphracts charged past their artillery-wielding counterparts. Prince Edval swung his war hammer at them in an awkward, backhand blow that still had enough force behind it to smash one of the attackers into the ground. Impossibly nimble for such a large machine, another of the multi-legged war engines scuttled up the haft of the *Queen Jeriel*'s weapon and pounced onto her shoulder. Savagely sharp pincers jammed into the gap between her pauldron and breastplate, and control cables snapped like broken violin strings. *Queen Jeriel*'s mighty arm went limp.

The crowd on the wall went quiet.

With surgical efficiency, more of the clawed Cataphracts moved in on the *Tender Mercy of Queen Jeriel*, dragging her to the ground. Another of the machines put its claws to the siegebreaker's visor and pried it open, while a third thrust its claw inside and plucked Prince Edval out of his helm-seat. With his bulky armor and windmilling limbs, the prince looked like a tick captured by a pair of tweezers and pulled free of its host. Despite the horror of the situation, Victor found himself impressed. That the Brethren's Cataphract was able to hold Prince Edval without crushing him was a telling indicator of how well it was constructed, and how well its captain was trained. The other crab-machines formed a line, leveling their cannons at Braveharbor's main gate to preempt any rescue attempts.

With Prince Edval captured, the clawed Cataphracts released their hold on the *Queen Jeriel* and started marching for the walls of the city. The Prince's captor led the formation, holding him aloft like a trophy. Prince Edval thrashed about, shouting demands and insults at his captors. As they got nearer, Victor recognized the Speaker riding on the back of the lead crab-machine, his gold chains and metal voice box glittering in the sun. The Brethren stopped at a musket shot's distance, directly in front of the main gate.

"People of Braveharbor, rejoice!" The Speaker's voice boomed out, easily overwhelming Prince Edval's defiance, making him seem childish and powerless in comparison. "You stand witness to a momentous day! We, the Brethren of the Chain, are generous enough, fortunate enough, to offer you the chance to join your links to ours! Your champion has failed you. He failed you the moment he took to the field to oppose us. As you have seen, our weapons are far superior to yours, and to raise arms against us is a wasteful folly. So, we ask you, we beg you, open your gates and submit! Welcome us, and I promise, you shall become valued, honored links in the Great Chain! But, if you choose poorly, you shall meet the same fate as your champion!"

The Speaker stopped talking. Filling the silence, Prince Edval's screaming grew shriller, more desperate. The crab-machine closed its pincer, and the prince's body hit the ground in two pieces. Horrified gasps and shouts of alarm rose up from the audience along the wall. Victor fought down the bile rising in his throat and looked away from the sight of the machine's red-stained claws. Lady Fenvale, meanwhile, kept her face hard and expressionless.

"You have been invited! You have been warned! Do not waste this opportunity, people of Braveharbor! I beg you, each and every one of you. Make the right choice." The Speaker's voice choked with unfeigned emotion.

"You have three days."

CHAPTER 17

An impromptu defense council gathered at the Bell and Kettle. Braveharbor Castle might have been larger and more defensible, but the inn was closer to the city wall and had a steady supply of alcohol. The innkeeper had fled, joining the panicked crowds trying to escape via the ships still in dock.

Lady Fenvale stood over a large, round table, talking quietly with Lieutenant Iral and *Major Simon*'s captain, one Baron Reed. Baron Halborn was back at the *Challenge*, watching the main gate in case the Brethren went back on their word. Once news got out where the city's Cataphract captains were meeting, other men and women began to trickle in, whether invited or not. Soldiers held their weapons close as they nursed mugs of the inn's dark beer, while ruffle-clad courtiers murmured among themselves, sharing and gathering gossip. Clutching a bundle of maps and documents, Victor weaved through the crowd, trying not to trip over scabbarded swords and dangling cloaks. Lady Fenvale presided over it with easy, assumed authority. She looked over as Victor got closer and made room for him to stand next to her at the main table.

"This is Chief Engineer Victor Brinden," Lady Fenvale introduced him. "He's seen more of the Brethren than anyone here, myself included. Moreover, I owe this man my life. Listen to what he has to say."

"Er, thank you, Countess." Victor set his papers down on the beer-stained wood of the table. He tried not to dwell on the number of eyes on him as he rolled out a map of Braveharbor and the surrounding area on the table. Thankfully, the map had the same effect on the officers as a fish did on cats, and the soldiers forgot about Victor entirely. He marked the positions of various Cataphracts with whatever he could lay his hands on: copper coins for the *Huntress*, *Challenge*, and *Major Simon*. Old corks for the Brethren's multi-legged machines. Half a walnut shell for what was left of the *Queen Jeriel*.

"By both numbers and sheer tonnage, the Brethren have the advantage. What's more concerning, however, is their mechanical capabilities. You've seen what they did to—what the Brethren are capable of. Their machines are more mobile than ours, and the simple fact that half of them are armed with cannon means they're operating on a tactical paradigm unlike anything any of us have ever faced before."

"They've got us by the balls, you mean." Baron Reed looked up at Lady Fenvale, an incongruously boyish blush on his cheeks. "Proverbially speaking, that is, Countess."

"No need to mince words, Baron." Lady Fenvale shook her head, grim. "I know how deep in the shit we are."

"I should hope you do, considering this is all your fault, Countess." A gap formed in the crowd, and Chamberlain Bouslet stepped forward, flanked by a pair of large men in palace guard uniforms. Even in the dim light of the Bell and Kettle's main room, the chamberlain's gilt-threaded finery nearly glowed, making him look all the more out of place. "You have no authority here, Countess Fenvale. You may be the Beasthunter-Errant, but it's clear we're not facing a Behemoth. Therefore, you are not in command. I would thank you to stop acting as if you were."

"Then who's in charge, then?" Lady Fenvale asked.

"With Prince Edval's death, his titles and possessions fall to his son, Duke Astello."

"Duke Astello isn't here," Lady Fenvale said.

"Which is why it falls on me, the prince's loyal servant, to take command in his absence." Chamberlain Bouslet puffed himself up, the ruffled silk of his doublet making him look like a fancy-but-irate chicken.

"And you have a plan?" Lady Fenvale said.

"As it would happen, I do," Chamberlain Bouslet said. "We shall send word to the capital of our predicament Once the king hears of how the Brethren killed his brother, he shall send an army to exact his royal vengeance."

"That'll take a hell of a lot longer than three days," Lady Fenvale said. "Assuming the Brethren don't capture your messengers while they're trying to get to Kingsforge."

"Then it is our duty to hold out as long as we can." The chamberlain nodded.

"Hold out? How? We don't have the equipment, the manpower, or the supplies for a siege."

"We shall consolidate our forces within the castle." Light glinted off the heavy signet ring on Chamberlain Bouslet's finger as he started pushing coins around the map. "Concentrate a select, elite force within the castle, and the Brethren shall not be able to overcome us."

Baron Reed furrowed his brow. "And anyone who's stuck in the city—"

"—shall be regrettable, but unavoidable, casualties of war," the chamberlain said. "Though even then, their sacrifice shall serve us. The more time the Brethren spend capturing them, the more time we have for reinforcements to arrive."

"It won't work," Lady Fenvale said. "You all saw how their machines can move. They'll climb over the walls like spiders, or use artillery to blow the main gate off its hinges. Or both. We can't hold the city walls, and we can't hold the castle, either."

"Then I expect you to sell your lives dearly," said Chamberlain Bouslet. "It is your duty to the kingdom."

"It's my duty to the kingdom to *win*, Chamberlain," Lady Fenvale said.

"How?" Chamberlain Bouslet snapped. "You just said the battle is hopeless."

"A defense is hopeless. Which means we have to go on the attack." As Lady Fenvale spoke, murmuring rippled through the inn.

"What makes you think you will succeed, where Prince Edval failed?" Chamberlain Bouslet's voice hitched with combined grief and anger.

"Because I'm not an idiot, for one," Lady Fenvale growled.

"How dare you!" The chamberlain's face flushed as red as his doublet, and spittle flew from his lips. "This … this woman speaks treason! She has brought nothing but failure and ruin since setting foot in Braveharbor, and now she slanders the memory of the prince? I demand her arrest!"

Instead of drawing her sword, as Victor expected (and feared), Lady Fenvale merely held both hands out to the chamberlain, wrists together. "Go ahead. Slap me in chains and throw me in the dungeon. In three days, the Brethren will have you all shackled next to me. If you're lucky." Lady Fenvale turned to Baron Reed, then to Lieutenant Iral, offering her wrists in mock surrender. "Unless you think Chamberlain Bouslet will save you?"

No one moved.

"That's what I thought." Lady Fenvale broke the ensuing silence.

"Ungrateful wretches, all of you." Chamberlain Bouslet shook his head. "You may rest assured, the king shall hear of your insolence."

"Fine," Lady Fenvale spat. "Go. Complain. Meanwhile, we'll do everything we can to make sure you stay alive long enough for His Majesty to hear your whining personally."

"I shall not forget this, Countess." The chamberlain retreated from the table, trying to draw up what remained of his dignity. His guards fell into step behind him, as did a few of the other courtiers and even a handful of soldiers.

"I don't expect you to." Lady Fenvale glared at the man until he left the inn.

"Bouslet has always been an ass," Baron Reed said. "But he made a good point. The *Queen Jeriel* is far stronger than either my *Major Simon* or your *Huntress*, but the Brethren still tore her to bits."

"Only because Prince Edval went out there alone."

"We only have three Cataphracts against their entire force," Baron Reed said.

"That may be, but we've still got an advantage."

"We do?" Victor blurted.

"Think about it." Lady Fenvale nodded. "Why did that metal-voiced bastard give us three days to surrender? Why not just one day? Why not an hour? He's stalling. Which means they've got something that will give them an edge, three days from now. Reinforcements, possibly. Or maybe that's how long it will take them to repair their ship. Or maybe they're putting together some bigger, more terrible weapon that we don't even know about yet. If we can strike before the three days are up, we could catch them off guard."

"Maybe." Baron Reed rubbed at his chin, still looking down at the map. "But even if we ambush the Brethren, how do we keep them from just gunning us down with their artillery?"

"By cooking up some surprises of our own," Lady Fenvale said.

"You have something in mind?" Lieutenant Iral's mug of beer stopped halfway to his mouth, and he arched a brow.

"As a matter of fact, I do." Lady Fenvale's lips pulled back into a wolfish grin as she turned to look at Victor. "And better yet, we've got just the man to build them."

Hammers clanged, men shouted, and the acrid smell of combustible chemicals wafted through the air. The *Huntress'* sword and the *Challenge*'s battle-axe sat upon specially designed frames, laid out horizontally so teams of smiths could hone the enormous blades with files and whetstones. Lady Fenvale inspected the weapons personally, nodded her approval, and then found Victor at the center of it all, directing work crews from one task to the next. He looked up from his handful of notes as the countess approached.

"They're not safe," Victor said, not for the first time.

"We're at war, Victor," Lady Fenvale said, not for the first time. "There's no such thing as safe."

Victor looked up at the *Huntress* and frowned. A long length of bronze pipe the diameter of Victor's palm had been lashed to each of the Cataphract's forearms, running from the elbow to just short of the wrist. It was an awkward addition to the already-patchwork machine, and the cabling that trailed from the closed-off end of the pipe made it look even more slapdash. Similar devices had already been attached to the *Major Simon*, while the *Challenge*'s crew set about fastening more of the thick brass pipes to her arms.

"If it doesn't explode." Victor looked at his sketches and wondered if it was too late to start over from scratch, or better yet, remove the damn things entirely. "On paper, the design is sound, but it'd be better if I had the time to run some tests—"

"It'd be better if we had General Barrowgale's squadron here to back us up, but there's no sense in getting worked up about it. Remember, we're only going to use them once." Lady Fenvale looked up at her Cataphract for a long, thoughtful moment, not at all put off by the *Huntress'* recent additions. "How do you use them, anyway?"

"If I had more time, I could have integrated the ignition device properly, but since I didn't, I had to make do with an external solution. See the rope coming out of the end, there?" Victor put his notes away and pointed to the length of taut hemp rope in question. "The other end's connected to a handle at the helm-seat. You'll recognize it. It's the red one that wasn't there before. Pull it once to prime the striker. Pull it again, and it'll shoot. Probably. Once you do, you can use the *Huntress'* sword to cut through the bindings and dump the empty pipe so it doesn't weigh you down. Just make sure you fire both tubes before you get stuck in. The lines are unprotected, so any blow to either arm would render the tubes unable to fire, or even set them off prematurely."

"I'll keep that in mind." Lady Fenvale nodded. "What about the other preparations?"

"That was just a matter of chemistry. It's a lot simpler than bolting experimental weaponry onto a Cataphract that was never meant to carry it in the first place." Victor took off his glasses and wiped the lenses with a scrap of cloth that had miraculously remained clean even after several hours of dirty, sweaty engineering work. "We should have everything ready by dark, so long as the Brethren don't attack before then." Victor's mouth dried up as he looked in the direction of the city wall. "They, uh, they're not going to attack before then, are they?"

"They haven't moved in on the city. Yet. The Brethren have set up camp around the *Queen Jeriel*, and they've got most of their machines bunched up on the other side, out of view. They're working on something, but I don't know what."

"I've been thinking about that." Victor slipped his glasses back on. "If their engineers are skilled enough, they might even try salvaging the *Queen Jeriel* and using her against us. Three days is enough time to get a Cataphract that size ... mostly functional. The Brethren used captured Cataphracts at the battle of Osterbridge. I wouldn't be surprised if they did so again."

"We're already outnumbered, but the *Queen Jeriel* would tilt the balance even more. Good thing we're attacking tonight." Lady Fenvale paused and took a deep breath. "Victor. There's one last thing I would ask of you."

"And that is?"

"Should I die here ... " Lady Fenvale produced an envelope with the *Huntress'* leaping-hound sigil pressed into the black wax of its seal. "Take Lily and get to safety. Once you do, I want you to deliver this to Lady Rosalind. Personally. It's ... an apology."

Victor stared at the envelope as if it were a lit alchemical furnace. "I—I couldn't. I mean, you won't. Die, that is. Will you? The whole point of all this—" He gestured to the bustling preparations all around him. "—was to make sure that you *did* survive."

"It's war, Victor. Nothing can be certain. I don't intend to die here, but it still pays to have … contingencies." She pressed the envelope against Victor's chest, forcing him to take it. "If I survive—"

"Which you will—"

"—burn the letter."

"I'll, uh, I'll look forward to it." The letter sat uncomfortably heavy in Victor's hands. "Your survival, that is. Not so much the burning."

"Then you'll do it?"

"Of course." Victor slid the envelope into his doublet and tried not to dwell on the stiff paper pressing against his chest. "But--"

"But?"

"I imagine that whatever sentiments you have in this letter would be better conveyed, er, in person? You know, when all of this is over with. I wouldn't presume to make any assumptions regarding your, er, personal affairs, much less your unique ... rapport with Lady Rosalind. But I am certain she would appreciate a first-hand apology far more than a posthumous one."

Lady Fenvale pursed her lips into a grim line as she ruminated over Victor's words. "You ... may be right, Victor," she said, begrudgingly, "but it's still good to have contingencies."

"The best contingencies are ones you never have to use," said Victor.

"And there you're *definitely* right." Lady Fenvale said.

"In any case, Lady Fenvale, let's hope that we won't need this letter at all." Victor nodded. "But, ah, might I ask a small favor?"

"Name it," Lady Fenvale said without hesitation.

"I didn't think to write a letter, but, should something ... unfortunate happen to me, would you find Marissa—er, Master Smith Chalment, and tell her—oh damn, do you think I've got time to write something?"

"You don't need to. You'll be safe behind the city walls—"

161

"About that."

"What?" Lady Fenvale said.

"I volunteered to ride with Lieutenant Iral."

"What."

"I'll be at the back, if that helps?"

"It doesn't." Lady Fenvale stared at Victor for a long, long moment. "I at least hope you have a reason you want to do something so bravely foolish?"

"I want to help." The words sounded childish and petulant as Victor said them.

"You are helping." Lady Fenvale waved a gloved hand at the bustle around the Cataphracts. "We both know you're better with a wrench than a sword."

"Which is why I need to be in the first wave," Victor said. "I want—I need to get a better look at the Brethren's machinery. Even if —when—we win here, it's only a matter of time before the Brethren field more of their new Cataphracts. Someone's got to get a look at them in action, to see what they're capable of. Someone who knows engineering. Preferably, someone who's at least had some experience with this sort of thing before. Moreover, who knows what new weapon they're working on. You might even have need of a saboteur."

"You don't have to prove anything, Victor." Lady Fenvale squeezed his shoulder, tight enough to bruise.

"Thank you," Victor said. "I appreciate that. But the fact of the matter still stands that I'm the best man for the job."

"You really are." Lady Fenvale's dark eyes bored into Victor's, and she nodded, releasing her grip, much to Victor's relief. "It's not a bad idea, to be honest. At least you told me first, instead of just stealing a horse at the last minute. Is there anything else you need to do here?"

Victor looked over the waiting Cataphracts again, watching the *Major Simon* and *Challenge*'s crews work. "Not at the moment, no. The installation is mostly complete—"

"Good," Lady Fenvale said. "That almost gives us enough time to get you properly dressed."

CHAPTER 18

"Properly" turned out to be a subjective term. The steel breastplate Lady Fenvale foisted on him sat heavily on Victor's shoulders. He twisted at the waist, testing the armor's flexibility--or lack thereof. His helmet was marginally better; the leather strap holding the brimmed steel cap in place dug into his chin, but Victor could at least turn his head without much trouble. At least it was just the helm and breastplate; Victor feared the weight of the full battle harness worn by the horsemen at the head of the column would render him immobile.

The *Huntress*, the *Challenge*, and the *Major Simon* waited behind Braveharbor's main gate, and their respective cavalry escorts milled about their ankles. They'd mustered nearly a hundred horsemen willing to fight the Brethren. It was more than Victor had expected--and yet it seemed like barely enough.

Victor looked down at his gear. A brace of wheel-lock pistols rested in their holsters, and a sack of improvised incendiaries hung off the right side of his saddle, easily within arm's reach. He hoped he wouldn't have to use either. Victor also carried a small selection of tools in a bag hanging at his left hip, in case he needed to make some battlefield repairs to the *Huntress*. He hoped he wouldn't have to use those, either, but the wrenches and pliers and so on were at least more familiar than the weapons and armor Lady Fenvale had given him.

Mimicking the more experienced cavalrymen, Victor wrapped a length of match cord around his left hand, thankful that his riding gloves fit better than his borrowed armor did. A young boy with soot-stained cheeks came by with an oil lantern, lighting each cavalryman's match cord. Soon, the nostril-searing smell of tar-soaked rope filled the gate plaza as the fuses glowed in the twilight like a row of tiny red stars.

Victor kept his hand held out to the side so a falling ember wouldn't fall onto his horse's coat, or worse yet, into the bag of firebombs hanging from the other side of the saddle. That part would come later.

Lady Fenvale opened the *Huntress'* visor and stood, surveying the assembled men. She'd changed into a fresh doublet with the *Huntress'* leaping-hound sigil shining bright in gold thread over her left breast. The countess' dark hair was tied back into a bun, though several strands had already pulled free to waft in the evening breeze. She held her saber in one hand and a speaking cone in the other.

"Ready?" Lady Fenvale called out. The *Major Simon* and *Challenge* saluted in reply, as did Lieutenant Iral and his men.

"Good! You all know what to do. Now, open the gates!" At her order, the towering doors swung inward, and the dragoons started moving. The column streamed out into the night in a thundering clamor of shouting men and pounding hooves. Victor spurred his own mount on, staying at the rear of the column as Lady Fenvale had told him to. Lily bounded along beside Victor's horse, unwilling to leave his side. As the cavalry rode through the main gate, Lady Fenvale leveled her sword at the men on the battlements. "Gunners, fire!"

Victor knew it was coming, but the boom of artillery still made him jump. The swivel guns mounted on the battlements weren't powerful enough to reach the Brethren's camp, but they didn't have to. Hollow lead balls, filled with a mixture of grease, lamp oil, and sawdust, hit the ground between Braveharbor's wall and the Brethren's position. The smoke bombs worked perfectly, clouding the air to block the sight of charging cavalry, if for just a few seconds. Dragoons at the head of the column lit and threw more smoke bombs for cover, only adding to the chaos.

In the distance, the Brethren moved to meet the attack.

Pulse pounding in his ears, Victor watched the massive shapes of the Brethren's machines silhouetted on the other side of the smoke curtain. Fire flared from the back of one such silhouette, and a cannon boomed. But with the smoke, the ball went wide and sent a geyser of dirt into the air, leaving the column untouched. A second cannon fired, and then a third. By luck or by skill, the third cannonball hit home, smashing men and horses into gory ruin. Victor leaned against the neck of his galloping horse, trying to present a smaller target.

The dragoons rode on.

Lieutenant Iral led the column straight into the Brethren's formation, weaving his mount between the scuttling legs of the crab-machines. The dragoons harried the Brethren's machines, firing pistols and lobbing firebombs. A detachment of cavalry surged ahead, past the Brethren's crab-machines and into their camp proper to burn tents and supplies. Victor drew one of his wheel locks and fired in the general direction of a Brethren Cataphract, but he couldn't tell if he hit anything. Amid the bomb bursts and pistol fire, Lily barked and snarled fearlessly, frustrated at the lack of any opponents within biting distance.

The design of the Brethren's Cataphracts worked against them; where the helm-seat of a standard duelist or siegebreaker was several stories above ground, the flatter, crablike structure of the Brethren's machines put their helms and gun crews within throwing distance. Red flame flared up when the bottles broke on the Cataphracts' metal hulls, and the artillery crews scrambled to put out the flames.

Victor stuffed his spent gun back into its holster and took one of the improvised grenades from his saddlebag. He managed to get it lit, only to fumble the bottle when the ground shook with the heavy steps of one of the clawed Cataphracts. The smoke bomb flared to life beneath the looming machine, and a cloud of choking smoke billowed upward. The Cataphract's visor popped open, and the Brethren at the helm hacked and coughed, trying to get a lungful of fresh air.

A dragoon rode up next to Victor and fired his wheel lock, putting a ball straight through the Brethren captain's skull. The dead man slumped down in his seat, and his Cataphract followed suit, its multiple limbs going slack without anyone to work the control levers.

166

"Got one!" The rider laughed madly and rode off into the smoke and chaos. No sooner had he disappeared into the smoke, three more clawed Cataphracts waded into the fray. They swept their pincers in wide arcs and sent dragoons and their mounts flying through the air like broken toys.

While the cavalry had caught the Brethren by surprise, the battle inevitably began to turn once the enemy regrouped. Victor hauled on the reins of his horse and fled from the assault. Behind him, a man's terrified scream was cut short by a sudden, grisly snap. Men fought. Shouted. Died. Close enough to tear into the horsemen, there was no question of which side would come out on top. Victor rode blindly through the smoke, until he found himself at the edge of the melee. He reached up to wipe tears and soot from his face, only to burn his cheek with the match cord still wrapped around his wrist. Victor yelped out an obscenity and threw the burning match cord to the ground. Lily, miraculously unhurt and still at Victor's side, leaned down to sniff curiously at it. Victor, meanwhile, could only sit in his saddle and watch the battle playing out around the dormant hulk of the *Tender Mercy of Queen Jeriel*.

The ground shook, jolting Victor out of his shocked stupor. Just from the familiar rhythm of the approaching footfalls, Victor knew their source without turning around in his saddle.

The *Huntress* had come to battle.

Lady Fenvale pushed her machine hard, outpacing the *Challenge* and *Major Simon* as she rushed across the battlefield as fast as she could go. She strode past Victor and Lily without slowing down and plunged into the fray, while one of the Brethren's artillery machines staggered out of the smoke to face her. The crew leader shouted once he saw the *Huntress*, and the men chained to the cannon frantically reloaded their gun. As fast as the *Huntress* could move, it was clear she wouldn't make it into sword range before they could fire.

She didn't have to.

The *Huntress* leveled her left arm at the artillery crew, and a moment later the firework rockets Victor had mounted to her arm ignited and streaked across the battlefield. The rockets burst on the artillery machine's hull; they didn't have enough of a charge to break through the steel plating, and weren't accurate enough to strike a weaker point such as a joint or an exhaust vent. But the re-purposed fireworks were loud and bright enough to make the gun crew chained to the cannon duck for cover.

And that was all the distraction the *Huntress* needed. She lunged forward and thrust her blade through a gap in the artillery Cataphract's visor.

A quick, efficient twist of the blade mangled the Brethren machine's helm-seat (and anyone sitting at it), and the *Huntress* yanked her sword free, just in time to parry the claws of one of the Brethren's heavier machines. The crab-machine clamped its pincers around the blade and pulled, but the *Huntress*' grip held. With her free hand, the white-armored duelist grabbed the cannon from the back of the downed artillery machine and yanked it from its mountings, shattering wood and breaking chain. Holding the cannon by the barrel, the *Huntress* used it to bludgeon the Brethren machine she grappled with, blow after hammering blow, until it fell to the ground with its visor staved in. No sooner had Lady Fenvale dispatched the first clawed machine, a second scrambled up to take its place. Metal plating crunched beneath its pincers as it dug into the *Huntress*' knee joint, and the white-armored duelist staggered.

Just from watching the *Huntress* move, Victor could tell the motive gear assembly in her knee was still intact (a lucky thing, too, considering the trouble they'd taken in stealing it). But the surrounding armor plates were bent inward, grinding against each other where they should have moved smoothly. And yet, the *Huntress* limped on, stubborn and unyielding. The *Huntress*' sword arm was still intact, and Lady Fenvale certainly put it to deadly use.

Moments later, the *Challenge* and the *Major Simon* entered the fray. As the other duelists threw themselves into the battle, they fired their own improvised rocketry-- or at least they tried to. Whether through a fault in the ignition mechanism, or improperly packed powder, or a weak point in the rocket's casing, the explosives mounted on the *Challenge*'s left arm backfired. Victor had feared such a catastrophic failure in the experimental weaponry-- though he felt a perverse sense of relief that it wasn't the *Huntress*' weapons that had failed.

The blast ripped through the *Challenge*'s elbow, severing the arm at the joint. The scorched remains of the duelist's forearm crashed to the ground, trailing lengths of control cable like severed tendons. Grievous as it was, the damage was at least localized; the core mechanisms within the *Challenge*'s torso remained intact. And so, she fought on, wielding her massive battle-axe with her remaining hand. The *Major Simon* moved to support her, standing at the *Challenge*'s right to keep any enemy from approaching her on her damaged side. Another of the crab-machines crouched low and sprang onto the *Major Simon*, slamming her onto her back. The *Huntress* closed her left hand around one of the crab-machine's scuttling legs and dragged it away from the *Major Simon*, then upended her sword to skewer it through the body. The *Major Simon* lumbered back to her feet, rejoining the other two duelists in battle.

It was a loud, chaotic, brutal fight-- just as Lady Fenvale had said it would be. Victor watched the battle play out from the sidelines, a single horseman (and a large dog) easily lost amidst the din of battle. The flame from burning Cataphracts lit the field with a hellish glow, and the stink of blood and gunpowder hung heavy in the air. Crab-machines soon surrounded the *Huntress* and her cohort, but harrying attacks from the cavalry kept the Brethren off balance, unable to organize a counterattack.

The *Huntress* lunged, skewering one of the artillery-machines with her sword before grabbing hold of the cannon's barrel with her free hand. Bolts snapped and metal splintered as the *Huntress* wrenched the gun free of its mounting, and the artillery crew scrambled away as their chains broke. Another Brethren Cataphract scuttled closer, claws grasping, until the *Huntress* struck it a backhanded blow, using the cannon as an impromptu bludgeon. Metal scraped on metal as the *Huntress* yanked her sword free and turned to face her next opponent.

Victor watched the battle play out, tracking the length of the *Huntress'* gait, the speed of her strikes, the amount of blue smoke pumping from her exhaust vents. The white armored Cataphract performed beautifully, every gear and cable moving in perfect unison. So long as the *Huntress* had Lady Fenvale at her helm, Victor knew there was nothing the Brethren could build that could face her.

Behind the fighting Cataphracts, The *Tender Mercy of Queen Jeriel* stirred to life.

A machine as large as The *Tender Mercy of Queen Jeriel* did not, could not, move quickly-- even activating her alchemical furnace was a slow and methodical process. But it was a process that had been started nonetheless, building in momentum with all the terrible inevitability of an oncoming thundercloud. By Victor's reckoning, the Brethren must have started getting her up and moving as soon as the first horsemen had sallied forth from Braveharbor's main gate. And so, the Siegebreaker lurched to her feet, hellishly lit by the fires blazing across the battlefield. The Brethren hadn't had the time to repair her fully. Gaps and rents in the *Queen Jeriel*'s armor revealed pistoning mechanisms and steadily growing plumes of blue alchemical smoke. But the Brethren had at least repaired her internals enough to get the siegebreaker moving-- and fighting. Even damaged, the sheer mass and strength of the *Queen Jeriel* could turn the tide of a battle.

Especially if she took her enemies by surprise.

Victor tried to shout a warning, but the din of clashing metal and screaming men easily drowned out his voice. He could only clench his fingers around his horse's reins as he watched the *Queen Jeriel* smash her enormous war-hammer into the *Major Simon*, downing the Duelist in a single blow. One of the Brethren's crab-cataphracts seized the opportunity, pouncing upon the *Major Simon* to pin her down as soon as the *Queen Jeriel* drew her hammer back. The *Queen Jeriel* lashed out with a clumsy backhand that only clipped the *Challenge*, but was still enough to send her staggering into the waiting claws of the Brethren's machines. The cavalry scattered and withdrew.

And just like that, the *Huntress* stood alone.

The *Queen Jeriel* swept her hammer in a wide, clumsy arc, but Lady Fenvale dropped the *Huntress* into a low crouch, allowing the blow to pass harmlessly overhead. Once the blow passed, the *Huntress* lunged forward, thrusting her sword into the inside of the *Queen Jeriel*'s wrist joint with surgical precision. Even across the battlefield, Victor could hear the telltale snap of severed control cables, and the *Queen Jeriel*'s heavy war-hammer slipped from suddenly-slack fingers. The *Queen Jeriel* awkwardly tried to adjust her grip, as even the siegebreaker's great strength struggled to wield such a heavy weapon one-handed.

The *Queen Jeriel*'s visor creaked open and revealed the Speaker, identifiable by his golden chains, standing behind the helm-seat. Thinner steel chains wrapped around the Speaker's waist, trailing down to a less-visible figure hunched over the controls, doing the actual work of operating the siegebreaker.

"You cannot win, Countess!" The Speaker's augmented voice carried even over the clamor and chaos of battle. "Even you can see you are outnumbered, outmatched! It pains me to see someone so brave, so fearless, throw their life away needlessly! But there is yet time! Surrender now, and you may yet live to become a valuable link in our chain!

Lady Fenvale didn't bother opening the *Huntress'* visor to reply. Instead, the *Huntress* dropped the cannon in her left hand, then raised it with metal fingers crooked into an unmistakable gesture: the drover's salute.

"Defiant to the last." The Speaker shook his head, rueful. "Such a waste! But, let it not be said that I did not give you every opportunity to better yourself. You have made your choice-- so perish!"

The Speaker yanked on the chains around his waist, and in turn the man at the *Queen Jeriel*'s helm pulled a lever to close the siegebreaker's visor. A second later, the enormous machine lunged forward, swinging her good hand at the *Huntress* in a sweeping punch. The *Huntress* ducked the awkward blow, then countered with a cut at the *Queen Jeriel*'s other wrist-joint. The blow threw up sparks as it glanced harmlessly from thick steel armor.

Tremors rumbled through the ground as the *Queen Jeriel* stomped forward, pressing her attack. The *Huntress* gave ground, backing away from her larger opponent. One of the remaining crab-machines that wasn't occupied with the *Challenge* or the *Major Simon* scuttled forward, claws snapping at the *Huntress'* flank. The *Huntress* batted the crab-machine's grasping claws away, then thrust her sword straight into the crab-machine's visor with deadly efficiency. Without breaking stride, the *Huntress* seized one of her opponent's suddenly-limp claws and heaved it in the path of the *Queen Jeriel*. Armor plating crumpled like mere foil beneath the siegebreaker's massive foot, but the *Queen Jeriel* didn't slow down.

The *Huntress* withdrew from the burning remnants of the Brethren camp, and the *Queen Jeriel* followed. Though dark, it was impossible to miss the movement of the hulking machines; Victor could nearly track them by the feel of their thunderous footsteps alone. With each stride, the *Huntress* led the *Queen Jeriel* farther from the walls of Braveharbor.

But to what end?

Victor worried at the inside of his cheek. In theory, Lady Fenvale could win. The *Huntress* took some damage in the battle, but she was still in better shape than the *Queen Jeriel*. Moreover, Victor had no doubt that Lady Fenvale was more skilled at helming her Cataphract than whoever the Speaker had picked to work the *Queen Jeriel*'s controls. On the other hand, the sheer, overwhelming mass of the *Tender Mercy of Queen Jeriel* made her dangerous. If the siegebreaker simply fell on the *Huntress*, it'd be enough to crush her. If Lady Fenvale missed just one step, or reacted just a second slower-- a single mistake would be all the *Queen Jeriel* needed to end the battle then and there, and render the *Huntress* nothing more but another broken husk, just like the other broken Cataphracts littering the battlefield.

And that's what gave Victor an idea.

"Lily, stay here." He said. "I'm about to do something very stupid."

The blazing flames of wrecked Cataphracts lit what was left of the Brethren's camp. In the shadows and chaos, none of the Brethren noticed him-- the few still functioning Cataphracts the Brethren had were busy in holding down the *Major Simon* and the *Challenge*. Victor spurred his horse on, winding his way through the churned earth and shattered Cataphracts until he found one machine in particular.

The crab-shaped machine was slumped forward, with its claws laying limp upon the ground. Its visor still yawned open, revealing her captain, shot dead at the helm-seat. Miraculously, there was no further damage to the Cataphract-- at least not that Victor could see. Lady Fenvale and her cohort must have stopped paying attention to the machine once it stopped moving, and the Brethren hadn't yet had the time to regroup and find someone else to man the controls.

Which meant the Cataphract was free for the taking.

Victor dismounted, then set his horse loose. After a moment's thought, he unbuckled the straps to his ill-fitting breastplate as well and discarded it. Now several pounds lighter, Victor climbed up the length of one of the Brethren machine's claws; it wasn't very different from scaling the *Huntress'* armor plates to make quick inspections. Hands held out for balance, Victor walked across the top of the crab-machine's hull, then swung down past her open visor with a minimum of flailing. Once inside, Victor set about dislodging the Cataphract's previous pilot without having to look at the ruinous wound in his face.

Instead of the leather straps and buckles that would secure someone in a proper Cataphract, the man was held in his seat by lengths of chain. Which, while thematically appropriate for the Brethren, still struck Victor as terribly inefficient. Instead of looking for a key or a mechanical release, Victor used a prybar to wrench the chain's anchor points loose. This done, he unceremoniously shoved the dead pilot out through the open visor and tried to ignore the heavy thump the corpse made when it hit the ground below. With the helm seat clear, Victor slid into place behind the controls and looked them over, identifying control levers, throttle valves, pressure gauges and all the other components necessary to the operation of a Cataphract. Their placement was far different from how the *Huntress* was designed, but there was still a certain logic to the layout.

A quick glance at the gauges verified that the Cataphract's alchemical furnace was still up and running, giving Victor enough power to start experimenting with the controls. Slowly, tentatively, he took hold of the largest control lever on his right and pushed it forward. As he did, the corresponding crab-claw matched the movement in a clumsy arc. A squeeze of the control lever's handle verified it operated the claw itself, which opened and shut at Victor's bidding.

Movement proved easier than expected-- there were only two pedals mounted on the floor. Victor had imagined some nightmare scenario of a pedal for each scuttling crustacean-modeled leg. He tested the pedals, soon deducing how they moved the crab-machine forward and backward. The legs must have been synchronized via some sort of cleverly designed gear mechanism. For a brief moment, Victor found himself giddily anticipating the chance to disassemble and examine the internal mechanisms inside of a proper workshop--

In the distance, steel struck steel.

"Right. Don't get distracted." Victor murmured, and steered the crab-machine towards the sound of battle. The scuttling gait of the multi-legged machine bounced the unpadded helm-seat up and down. Unsurprisingly, the Brethren hadn't designed their Cataphracts for comfort. Victor clung to the controls, gritting his teeth together so he wouldn't bite his tongue by accident, and pressed on. With the throttle valves open all the way, it didn't take long for Victor to close in on the *Huntress* and the *Queen Jeriel*. Lady Fenvale still kept her larger opponent at bay, by turns retreating and attacking whenever the *Queen Jeriel* was off balance. The *Huntress'* broadsword cut and thrust, seeking out gaps in the siegebreaker's thick armor. In turn, the *Queen Jeriel* swiped and grabbed at the *Huntress*, only for the quicker machine to dodge and slip away. Clear from the smoke and chaos of the battle, the two machines were lit by moonlight, giving the duel an eerie, otherworldly air. Neither Cataphract reacted to Victor's approach-- which was exactly what he was counting on.

With his heart in his stomach, Victor opened the throttle all the way, and his stolen Cataphract barreled into the back of the *Queen Jeriel*'s legs. Up so close, Victor could see the intricate scroll work engraved into the *Queen Jeriel*'s armor, marred by the dents and holes from when the Brethren had initially overwhelmed and captured her. Victor yanked on the control levers, and the Crab-Cataphract's claws dug into the metal plating of the *Queen Jeriel*'s thigh, and an ear-punishing screech echoed out into the night. He feverishly worked the controls, gouging deeper with the crablike claws, pushing past the armor plating to get at the *Queen Jeriel*'s knee joint. If he could cripple her before--

A sudden, unexpected jolt shook every bolt and plate of Victor's crab machine. He looked up through the holes of the visor just in time to see the *Queen Jeriel*'s enormous hand swinging down for a second blow. Victor's Cataphract shook again, and he felt the control lever in his left hand go slack-- the cabling or motive gears that operated one of the claw arms must have been damaged. The *Queen Jeriel* landed a second blow, and the crab machine listed to the left as several of her legs crumpled. Catastrophic as the damage was, Victor knew it could've been worse: with better leverage and her hammer in hand, the *Queen Jeriel* could have shattered his Cataphract with a single blow. Victor looked up, through the slotted visor, and watched the *Queen Jeriel* raise her fist again, and with a sinking certainty, Victor knew he wouldn't survive another hit. He closed his eyes and breathed in deeply, preparing himself for his painful, messy demise.

Which was all hell broke loose.

Again.

The *Huntress*' white armor gleamed in the moonlight as she lunged forward. With savage efficiency, she thrust the point of her broadsword into the *Queen Jeriel*'s armpit, neatly sliding the blade between the thicker armor plating to mangle the more delicate mechanisms within. The siegebreaker staggered, already off balance from Victor's attack. With the slow inevitability of a felled oak, the *Queen Jeriel* toppled backwards. Victor wrestled with his machine's unresponsive controls, trying vainly to get out of the way, but then came an eardrum-punishing crash, and everything went dark.

Victor surprised himself by waking up.

One by one, Victor registered individual, disconnected sensations. The acrid smell of alchemical smoke leaking into the cockpit. The rhythmic tick of some shattered mechanism still vainly attempting to function despite the catastrophic damage. The wet, warm drip of blood trickling down his forehead.

And pain.

Every part of his body ached-- Victor tried to look at it optimistically; each part of him that hurt was a part that was still attached. And everything hurt. He blinked his eyes open to find himself still at the helm-seat of his stolen Cataphract, though the entire machine was slanted several degrees to the left. Victor blundered around in the dark until he found the lever that opened the machine's visor. Cool night air flowed into the helm-seat, and Victor climbed out of the ruined machine. Victor's bruised, stiff limbs made the going difficult, but he managed to crawl out without breaking anything that wasn't already broken. With his boots on the ground, Victor was able to look up and survey the scene.

The *Queen Jeriel* was sprawled out on her back, defeated, her arms and legs askew. One of the siegebreaker's legs pinned Victor's cataphract in place, the *Queen Jeriel* having done more damage in falling on the crab machine than it had done with its awkward punches from before. Swiftly growing blue flames flared up from gaps and holes in the crab machine's armor; Victor realized he'd gotten out just in time to avoid getting burned by the uncontrollable flames of a cracked alchemical furnace.

The *Huntress* still stood tall above the downed machines, alchemical flamelight reflecting of her white armor-- or at least the few patches of white that hadn't been scuffed, scraped, or dented over the course of the last several days.

Victor waved.

The *Huntress'* visor opened, and Lady Fenvale leaned out of her helm-seat. "Damnation, Victor, is that you?" Without waiting for a reply, Lady Fenvale eased her Cataphract into a kneeling position, then tossed out a rope ladder. She scrambled down from her helm-seat, then rushed over to where Victor stood.

"Victor, you brilliant idiot. I should have known you'd try something like that."

"That makes one of us." Victor smiled, even as Lady Fenvale clapped him on his freshly-bruised shoulder. "But I'll try to leave the piloting to you in the future."

"Fair."

"What sentimental nonsense." A hollow voice rasped from behind them. Lady Fenvale and Victor spun around, as the Speaker emerged from the shadow of the *Queen Jeriel*. His robes were torn, and the metal box set into his chest was dented, but the twin-barreled pistol he held looked entirely too functional. Keeping the weapon pointed at Victor and Lady Fenvale, he shuffled forward, dragging the limp body of one of his officers, still connected by the chain around his waist. He stopped a short distance away-- far enough to keep out of sword's reach, but close enough that a pistol shot wouldn't miss.

"Given the circumstances, yes." Lady Fenvale stepped in front of Victor, hand falling to her saber's hilt. "Now put that gun down before I have to kill you."

"My life is insignificant in the grander scheme of things." The Speaker's voice crackled through the damaged box in his chest. "There will be more after me. The Brethren of the Chain cannot, will not be stopped until we have united all the peoples of the world under our guidance."

"Let them come. I'll beat them just as I've beaten you." Lady Fenvale narrowed her eyes. Behind her, Victor tried to keep his panic in check, wishing he'd thought to bring a pistol of his own. He looked around, searching for something, anything that could be turned to their advantage, but found himself empty handed.

"Not if I kill you first." The Speaker leveled his pistol at Lady Fenvale's chest. "You have proven yourself a formidable foe, Countess. Which is why you must die, for the greater good of civilization. Without you to oppose them, my fellow Brethren will inevitably prevail, and your precious kingdom shall be just another link in the great chain of progress." The Speaker's voice grew more fervent, and his eyes gleamed with fanatic zeal.

"Kill me, and you won't live to see it. My men will run you down as soon as they hear the shot." As if to prove her point, hoofbeats sounded in the distance as Lieutenant Iral rallied his surviving men.

"Then I shall make martyrs of us both. Any last words, Countess?"

"Just two." Lady Fenvale tensed. "Lily, now!"

At the command, the dog sprung from where she'd crouched in the shadows behind the Speaker. She clamped her jaws down on his gun arm, and the crack of bone was soon followed by the crack of the pistol discharging into the ground. Despite the flash and noise of the gunfire, Lily held on, growling ferociously. Lady Fenvale sprung forward only a moment after Lily did. She drew her saber in a single, smooth motion and cut the Speaker down with a single stroke. The Speaker's body dropped to the ground, and his head rolled away.

"Good girl, Lily." Lady Fenvale planted the tip of her saber into the ground and whistled a quick command. Lily immediately dropped the Speaker's arm and bounded over to greet her owner, tail wagging. The Countess rewarded Lily with a scratch behind the ears, and then looked back at Victor. "Good idea, bringing the dog with you."

"I, er, told her to stay put, actually."

CHAPTER 19

The rest was cleanup.

With the Speaker dead and the *Tender Mercy of Queen Jeriel* defeated, the remaining Brethren of the Chain more inclined towards survival than fanaticism surrendered. Lieutenant Iral and his dragoons rounded the prisoners up, and crews of laborers from the city set out to clear the fields outside Braveharbor's walls of bodies and debris.

Some days later, Victor once again found himself inside a Brethren Cataphract, though under far more controlled conditions. He leaned into the half-disassembled machine, studying the tangle of motive gears and control cables that drove its many legs. Or used to, at least-- with the damage it had taken, Victor doubted the crab machine would ever scuttle again. But, even in a broken, crippled state, the Cataphract still provided a fascinating learning opportunity. The mechanisms were similar enough that Victor could understand what they were for, but they were all laid out in a completely different manner in order to facilitate multi-legged movement.

"I should have known I'd find you here." Marissa had to raise her voice to be heard above the din of clattering hammers and whirring machinery of Braveharbor's Cataphract yard. Victor took care not to hit his head as he climbed out of the Brethren Cataphract.

"Marissa!" Victor waved. "What are you doing here?"

"As soon as I heard the *Huntress* had fought off a whole invasion, I attached myself to the squadron escorting Duke Astello back here. Once we got close enough I borrowed a horse and rode ahead-- *King Leopold's Pardon* and company should arrive sometime this afternoon. I figured I could help you get the *Huntress* looking her best before they got here."

"Sorry to disappoint, but I've finished repairing her yesterday. For the most part, at least. She needs another coat of paint, and her sword could stand another pass with a whetstone, but other than that, the *Huntress* is in fine a shape as she's ever been."

"So you're sure there's not anything I can do?" Marissa affected a melodramatic pout. "After I've come all this way?"

"Oh! I didn't mean anything of the sort." Victor stammered. "In fact, I always appreciate your company-- and your expertise even more. It's just--"

Before he could stammer any further, Marissa grabbed a handful of Victor's grease-streaked shirt and pulled him down into a brief but no less enjoyable kiss. Once she leaned away, Victor smiled the dopey smile of the freshly kissed, then self-consciously wiped his soot-stained hands on his trousers. Marissa trailed gloved fingertips down Victor's chest, uncaring of the numerous stains he'd accrued over the last few hours. Instead of being put off by Victor's more-disheveled-than-usual appearance, she stepped in closer. Marissa's tongue traced briefly over her teeth, and she spoke the five most enticing words Victor had ever heard from a woman.

"What are you working on?"

Victor beckoned Marissa closer to the crab-machine he'd been disassembling. "Take a look. I don't know if I can repair any of these Cataphracts-- or even if I want to --but they're still fascinating. Whoever designed these Cataphracts must have been mad. Or a genius. Or both. Look at how they arranged the motive gears. They're even more intricate than I thought."

"It'd have to be." Marissa gently but firmly pushed Victor to the side so she could get a better look at one of the damaged Cataphract's splayed-out legs. "Bipedal motion is hard enough, but they're working on a completely different body scheme. Coordinating all those limbs to move in the right order makes it even easier for something to go wrong."

"Exactly! But they've built an array of counterweights around the motive gears that balance and distribute weight between the multiple legs automatically, which results in a far stabler platform. It might not have the reach or leverage that our Cataphracts do, but when you mount a cannon on the back, that doesn't matter. But what's even more interesting is the power system; the Brethren connected their alchemical furnaces differently than we do, but I haven't been able to place my finger on why. Which is why I've spent the last few hours stripping the machine down, piece by piece. Would you like to see my notes?"

"Victor, you sure know how to charm a lady." Marissa went over to the table where Victor had been storing his diagrams and shuffled through the papers, taking care not to smudge the still-drying ink. "So how close are you to the furnace?"

"I was just about to remove it, actually."

"Well, what are we waiting for?" Marissa set the notes down and rubbed her hands together. "Let's get to it."

"Could you hand me a wrench?"

Marissa obliged. Bolt by bolt, Victor worked his way deeper into the crab-machine. A second set of hands made the work go far faster, and more pleasantly, to boot. Every so often, Victor clambered out of the machine, getting out of the way so Marissa could get a better look at the complex machinery within. She kept herself mostly clean, staining her fingers more with ink than engine grease as she took notes of her own. After another half hour's work, Victor eased the alchemical furnace from its mounting. The outside of the stony nodule was rougher than any other furnace Victor had worked on before, and its shape was off--not quite perfectly spherical. Marissa cleared a spot on the workbench for Victor to set the cool furnace down, and the two of them peered at it. Unconsciously, the two alchemical engineers drifted closer and closer to each other as they hunched over the inert furnace. After several moments' examination, Marissa was the first to speak.

"Is that--"

"It is," Victor said. The anticipatory flush in his cheeks gave way to a shocked white.

Marissa frowned. "But that's--"

"Impossible, yes." Victor pushed his glasses further up his nose and hunched over the alchemical furnace to verify his findings. "We've got to tell Lady Fenvale--"

"Tell me what?" The Countess strolled into the Cataphract yard, sword at her hip and Lily on her side. She took in the sight of the two alchemical engineers standing so close together, and arched an eyebrow. "Not that it's any of my concern, but I think it's too soon to start thinking about ... nuptials."

"What? No, that's not it at all." Victor said-- and then looked over at Marissa. "Not that, er, such an idea isn't an appealing one, but--"

Marissa elbowed Victor in the side. Hard. "Show her the furnace."

"Ah, yes. Right. This is the alchemical furnace we took out of the Brethren's Cataphract." Victor nodded over his shoulder to the half-disassembled crab machine.

"And?" Lady Fenvale leaned over the workbench and peered at the chunk of stone and the tangle of valves and piping wrapped around it.

"It doesn't have a sigil." Victor said. "Every alchemical furnace that's ever come out of Kingsforge is stamped with a sigil to show which family has rightful claim to it."

"So the Brethren must have pried the thing off when they stole it however many years ago." Lady Fenvale said.

"That was my first thought as well. But I can't find any spots where bolts were set into the surface to indicate there was ever a sigil there to begin with. Moreover, the color's all wrong. I think the green tint is from some sort of copper content in its mineralogical composition, which is unlike any alchemical furnace either of us have ever seen." Victor looked at Marissa, who nodded in agreement.

Lady Fenvale frowned, taking a step back from the workbench. "So you're saying this didn't come from Kingsforge."

"That's my current hypothesis, yes," said Victor.

"Which means the Brethren have found a new source of alchemical furnaces." Lady Fenvale frowned.

"Also my current hypothesis," said Victor.

Lady Fenvale stared at the green-tinted alchemical furnace and tapped a finger on her saber's pommel, as if debating whether or not she could resolve the problem through swordplay. "Have you told anyone else about this?"

"Not yet, no."

"Then we'd should be the ones to deliver the news to the king directly." Lady Fenvale nodded, resolute. "Prepare that furnace for travel, Victor. Tomorrow, we march for Kingsforge."

FREE STORY!

ON THE VIRTUES OF A FINE CLOAK

On a cold winter's night, Lady Diana Fenvale must trek through the factory-city of Kingsforge to rescue her friend Sophia from the clutches of a boorish scoundrel. But once found, will Sophia even want to be rescued? By the end of the night, cards will be played, banter will be bandied, and steel will be drawn in ON THE VIRTUES OF A FINE CLOAK, a prequel to THE CATAPHRACT OATH!

Available for FREE to anyone who joins my mailing list!

https://marcedmondbest.carrd.co/

About the Author:

Marc Edmond Best grew up watching giant robot cartoons and movies with lots of sword fights in them, which explains a lot. He currently lives in St. Louis with his family and a dog not as brave but just as spoiled as the one in his novel.

https://marcedmondbest.carrd.co/